When Carol, David and Aunt Sarah came back from Sybil's, darkness was falling. While Aunt Sarah organized David into a bath before dinner, Carol listened to the one message on the answering machine.

The same whispered voice as before admonished her: *You haven't been paying attention, Carol Ashton. It was an accidental overdose. Why not just say that or do you want everyone to know what you and Sybil Quade do in bed? Collis Raeburn's death was an accident. Make sure your report says that.*

Aunt Sarah came hurrying back into the kitchen area. "Who was that?"

Carol was horrified to hear a shake in her voice as she said, "It's just a rather well-mannered anonymous call trying to persuade me that Collis Raeburn accidentally killed himself...This one's polite to an extraordinary extent, considering that he, or she, is threatening me."

Aunt Sarah looked alarmed. "Threatening you with what? Physical harm?"

It was hard to say the words. "Just exposure as a lesbian, Aunt. Just that."

DEAD CERTAIN
CLAIRE McNAB

The Naiad Press, Inc.
1992

Printed in the United States of America on acid-free paper
First Edition

Edited by Katherine V. Forrest
Cover design by Pat Tong and Bonnie Liss
    (Phoenix Graphics)
Typeset by Sandi Stancil

Library of Congress Cataloging-in-Publication Data

McNab, Claire
    Dead certain / by Claire McNab.
        p.   cm.
    ISBN 1-56280-027-2 : $9.95
    I. Title.
PS3563.C3877D38   1992
813'.54—dc20
                                                        92-18092
                                                             CIP

For my dear friend Sue

Acknowledgments

To: Katherine V. Forrest

W. Somerset Maugham said: "There are three rules for writing the novel. Unfortunately, no one knows what they are."
I know one vital rule—have a *great* editor. I have.

Thanks to:

Robin—for hotels;
Barbara—for opera.

ABOUT THE AUTHOR

Claire McNab is the author of the Detective Inspector Carol Ashton mysteries, *Lessons in Murder, Fatal Reunion, Death Down Under* and *Cop Out.* She also authored *Under the Southern Cross,* a romance. She firmly believes that every person should explore the beauties of Australia for herself and find out if Aussies really do say, "G'day!"

PROLOGUE

The young Duty Manager looked at the DO NOT
DISTURB sign, cleared his throat, straightened his
tie. He glanced at the substantial figure of the
Housekeeping Supervisor, who stopped chewing her
gum long enough to say, "Go for it."

"I can hear something. Someone talking."

"The television's on."

He paused a moment longer, then knocked
resolutely. "Mr. Raeburn? This is the Duty
Manager . . ."

The Housekeeping Supervisor sighed. "Hasn't

answered any of my room attendants. Not going to answer you."

"Mr. Raeburn . . . ?"

The television blared as he opened the door to a wall of cold air. He walked down the short entrance hall and stopped. "Jesus."

Collis Raeburn lay sprawled on the bed, his head turned away as though hiding his face. One arm hung over the edge so that his hand touched the plush beige carpet near an overturned tumbler and a scatter of pills. There was a pungent stink of whiskey.

Reluctantly, the Duty Manager touched his shoulder, then his face. "Jesus," he said again.

The Housekeeping Supervisor killed the television.

In the silence her matter-of-fact voice was too loud. "Offed himself." When the young man beside her didn't respond, she added, "Get the Manager and don't touch anything."

"Do you know who this *is*? Collis Raeburn, the opera singer."

The Housekeeping Supervisor was already walking towards the door. "Yeah? Whoever he is, he's still just as dead."

CHAPTER ONE

Lounging in the doorway of the office kitchen, Detective Sergeant Mark Bourke ran a hand over his freshly close-cropped brown hair. "It'll be quite a big wedding, actually. We both wanted something quiet, but Pat's got all these relatives..."

"It's not a good sign, lots of relatives," said Constable Anne Newsome dolefully as she spooned instant coffee into a mug.

Detective Inspector Carol Ashton, amused at the young constable's mockingly lugubrious tone, said,

"Anne could be right, Mark. Think of all those relations you're about to suddenly acquire, each asking for a traffic ticket to be fixed."

"I'll cope."

Smiling affectionately at his familiar, blunt-featured face, she was sure that he would. Mark Bourke met life with an equanimity firmly based upon a dry sense of humor and an aptitude for the sheer grind that made up so much of police work. Carol had worked with him on many cases, and by now they shared a respect and affection for each other that was never verbalized, but comfortingly, was always there.

"The wedding will be outside," he was saying. "Not a church. We're having a marriage celebrant. Hope the weather's okay—spring can be a bit dicey."

"Making up your own vows?"

Mark looked astonished at the constable's question. "Own vows? Pat never mentioned—"

"You can make up the whole thing. The only legal bit is when you sign your life away."

Carol thought of her own large, ostentatious society wedding to barrister Justin Hart at the very exclusive St. Mark's at Darling Point, and the civilized, quiet divorce some years later. "Thought you'd go for a formal wedding, Mark."

"I would have, Carol, believe me. You know I like everything set out, so I know where I am. But Pat wanted it at Balmoral Beach."

Anne chuckled. "On the sand, or ankle-deep in the water near the shark net?"

Carol looked at her reflectively as Mark described how the ceremony would be in the rotunda—a restored Victorian bandstand that sat fetchingly in a park near the creamy sand.

Top of her class at the Academy, ebullient, intelligent, Anne had been part of the team for over six months, and she had fitted in effortlessly. She volunteered her opinion, didn't seem awed by the other detectives, yet never presumed a status she didn't hold. Carol's initial antagonism was based, she had finally realized, on her chagrin that the cozy professional relationship she had enjoyed with Mark Bourke now had to accommodate an ambitious female officer. Anne Newsome's professionalism, however, had finally won Carol's reluctant approval, and then her support.

"Inspector Ashton?"

Carol turned to the gray-suited, sleek man who had uttered her name with soft emphasis. "Yes?"

He extended a hand. "I'm Simon Sykes, from the Commissioner's office. We haven't met before, Inspector, but I've admired your work for some time."

Public relations, thought Carol as they shook hands briefly.

"Is there somewhere we could talk?

Carol indicated her office. She closed the door before he could suggest it, then gestured him to a chair. He was neat, alert and deferential. Instinctively, Carol disliked and mistrusted him, but she smiled and said, "Yes, Mr. Sykes?"

"*Simon*—please. I'm with the Commissioner's press unit."

Carol nodded. *And you can call me Inspector Ashton.* She said, "You've just joined the unit?"

5

"Yes. My background's in public relations ..." A carefully self-deprecatory smile, then he went on smoothly, "The Commissioner's asked me to brief you before he sees you himself. There's a slight problem."

Police public relations had always presented challenges, especially in the past, when the Service had been the subject of several judicial inquiries into links between crime figures and senior police officers. A new Commissioner, a stringent cleansing of the ranks and a deliberate campaign to improve the Force's image had largely restored public confidence. The recent advent of a particularly ambitious and abrasive minister to the Police portfolio had resulted in a new drive for favorable publicity and further expansion in the PR area. The word had come down to maintain a high, positive profile for the Service, ostensibly to enhance the standing of police officers in general. The more cynical regarded the new emphasis as an effort to reinforce the new Police Minister's credentials as a future State Premier. Carol felt the choice of Senator Marjory Quince was a sound one, but she was also aware that, as a woman in what had previously been regarded as a man's job, it was likely the Senator felt constrained to appear more hard line than any previous incumbent.

"Just what is this slight problem?" Carol said briskly.

"It's the Raeburn death. The Commissioner wants you to take over the investigation."

There was no need for him to explain Collis Raeburn's identity. Since the discovery of his body in a five-star hotel two days before, the media had

6

thrashed around trying to create much out of the little that they could glean. Headlines such as AUSTRALIA'S PAVAROTTI DEAD vied with GOLDEN THROAT FOREVER HUSHED, and AUSTRALIA'S SONG IS ENDED. Television stations changed schedules to replay some of Collis Raeburn's greatest singing triumphs, particularly scenes from *Great South Land,* in which Raeburn had been depicted singing a variety of songs and arias at various landmarks—"Nessun Dorma" at night on a floodlit Ayers Rock, "The Flower Song" from *Carmen* at the tip of Cape York, and as a spectacular finale, "Advance Australia Fair" from the top of the arch of the Sydney Harbour Bridge.

Carol said, "Why am I to take over the case? I understand it looks like a straightforward suicide. Nothing suspicious."

Sykes checked the door was shut, then said in a low confidential tone, "Collis Raeburn was HIV-positive, and it wasn't from a blood transfusion."

HIV-positive. The phrase evoked a kaleidoscope of images and feelings: the fine-drawn features of a dying friend; bravery and grief; the pity and love on some faces, the hatred and fear on others . . .

"The family want it hushed up," said Sykes.

"You don't need me for that."

"There's more. The Raeburn family are insisting it's an accident. Not suicide."

Carol remained silent. She was used to being wheeled in when something requiring delicate handling of the media was required. Cynically, she ticked off her advantages: she was telegenic, she'd cultivated a network of useful media contacts, and

7

she'd learned the hard way to develop a cool, authoritative persona to deal with the most difficult of interviewers and the thorniest of questions.

"Insurance is involved," said Sykes. "If it's an accident, the company pays. If it's suicide . . ."

Carol's tone was tart. "This seems outside the scope of any police inquiry. We're required to compile a report for the coroner, that's all."

Sykes spread his hands. "The Raeburns are personal friends of the Police Minister." He waited for a response. Carol looked at him, feeling a shaft of disappointment that one of the few women to gain ministerial rank was demanding special favors like any other venal politician.

Sykes cleared his throat, leaned forward conspiratorially. "You know how it is. Just between us, the Commissioner's been asked to expedite the inquiry, keep any embarrassing details quiet, and get the case in front of the coroner as quickly as possible."

"Why me?"

Sykes smiled warmly. "Because you're the best, Inspector. That's why."

The Commissioner's palatial office seemed too glossy and slick for his hulking body and forthright personality. He frowned heavily at Sykes, who stood obsequiously to one side, then he looked back at Carol. "I don't like this any more than you do, Carol, but the Minister's insisting on special treatment."

Before she had left her office, Carol had spoken

briefly to the officer in charge of the initial investigation of Collis Raeburn's death. She said now, "There don't appear to be any suspicious circumstances. Although there's no note, everything points to suicide. In fact, he seems to have followed instructions from *The Euthanasia Handbook.* You're aware a copy was on the bedside table. And if Raeburn was HIV-positive, perhaps that, plus other pressures, led him to take his own life."

"His father and sister are adamant that there's no way he'd do that."

Skyes intervened. "The sleeping pills were prescribed. The family insist it's a tragic accident."

Carol felt a thread of impatience, but she was careful not to let it show. "My suggestion is that we expedite the report to the coroner, and let him rule on the matter."

Sykes stated authoritatively, "The media's a problem—"

The Commissioner interrupted. "The Minister's concerned about adverse publicity."

Sykes said smoothly, "Absolute discretion is required, of course."

The Commissioner flashed him a look of active dislike. "That was an unnecessary comment, Sykes. Inspector Ashton is quite aware that any mention of Raeburn's HIV status will be on a strict need-to-know basis."

Sykes, unabashed, straightened his tie. "I meant lower-ranked officers. Not Inspector Ashton. I'm sure you'll agree anyone working on the case must be specifically instructed."

"Yes. Yes," said the Commissioner impatiently. He leaned his bulk back in his chair. "Carol, you're to

9

head the investigation and take whatever damage control measures are necessary. You've got good relations with the media and I expect you to use them. Don't need to tell you what will happen if Raeburn's HIV status gets out. We want to spare the family that."

Carol wanted to say with bitter sarcasm, *Why not advise the family to pretend the virus was medically acquired? That'll gain shocked sympathy, not loathing and disgust . . .*

Sykes was saying smoothly, "It would be better for everyone if it's kept quiet. And the general public don't want to know about his private life, do they? Destroy an image. I mean, Collis Raeburn was practically an icon. Yes?"

Carol's opinion of the public was less charitable. People had a voracious appetite for any titillating scandal, and if Australia's golden-voiced tenor had secrets to hide, his public would consider it only fair that these should be revealed for everyone's shocked appreciation.

The Commissioner smoothed his trademark bushy eyebrows with a forefinger. "Carol, what's your caseload at the moment?"

"It's okay. I'll get onto Raeburn straight away."

"I want this quick, neat and tidy. And I'll have a word with your Chief Inspector . . . I want you reporting direct to me on this. Any problems, I want to hear about them. Right?" As she nodded, he added curtly, "Need Sykes?"

Carol was just as straightforward. "I don't think so."

"If you do, there's no problem. The Minister's pushing for this to be tied up as soon as possible.

You'll need to talk to Raeburn's family, but leave it until you've had time to get on top of everything before you contact his father or sister."

Sykes insisted on shaking hands with her again at the office door, holding the clasp just a little too long. "If I can be of assistance in some way, then you must call on me, Inspector, at any time."

She gave him a cool, level glance. "Thank you, Mr. Sykes."

"At any time . . ."

Mark Bourke was amused when she came into his spartan office to tell him about the meeting. "Don't want to hurt your feelings, Carol, but bringing *you* in to handle a probable suicide will almost certainly make the media wonder why. And that's what they're trying to avoid, isn't it—an investigative journalist or two sniffing around?"

"The Commissioner commands, I follow."

"Wise career move."

"Mark, does Pat move in opera circles?"

He couldn't prevent an indulgent smile. "My Patricia? Her position at the Art Gallery certainly puts her in with the in-crowd. Part of her job, if nothing else. You looking for some background?"

"Background, gossip—anything. And I'm interested in the Raeburn family, the father and daughter. Tell Pat it's quite unofficial. I just want her general impressions."

He leaned back and put his hands behind his head. "Plus who's doing what to whom?"

She matched his grin. "That too, of course." Her

smile faded as she thought, *Unknowingly infecting each other?* She said, "Until he had a blood test it seems clear Raeburn wasn't aware he could be passing the HIV virus to sexual partners."

Bourke rubbed his chin thoughtfully. "If he was having unprotected sex . . ." He grimaced. "Unless he told them after he got the results, there's some very bad news waiting for a few people, and if we follow orders, we can't even drop a broad hint."

"But, Mark," she protested, "if he *has* infected someone, then that person can be passing it on to someone else. This isn't herpes we're talking about, it's the very real chance of getting AIDS." When he didn't look impressed, she went on, "You know it's not an exclusively homosexual disease. Anyone can be at risk."

"I don't need a lecture," he said, half-smiling to ease the impact of his words.

But Carol, with a jolt, realized he had, in effect, chastised her. Normally she would have attempted a witty but sharp rejoinder. The sudden tension between them puzzled her. She chatted for a few moments to reestablish their usual relationship, then went back to her office.

Anne Newsome was waiting for her. "Here's the result of the post mortem and the preliminary report."

"Have you read it?"

"Yes. I glanced through it."

"Good. Since I won't have Mark exclusively on this—he'll be tying up the odds and ends of a few outstanding items in my caseload—I'll need you to assist me, especially with the interviews."

Carol couldn't miss Anne's faint flush of pleasure,

but the young constable maintained an appropriately professional air. "I took this message for you."

Carol frowned at Anne's neat, rounded writing. "Graeme Welton?"

"He called a few minutes ago. Said it was urgent."

"I'll call him." As Anne turned to go, she added, "I want you to check out Collis Raeburn's finances—any debts he had, what he did with his money. If you need any help, ask Mark."

Alone, Carol leaned back in her chair to consider the message from Graeme Welton. An avant-garde composer, he basked in publicity and had a talent for self-promotion. His most recent work, *The Sardonic Song of the Computer*, a full-length oratorio with God played by a super-computer, had not only jangled critics' musical sensibilities and outraged organized religion in general, but had also upset computer aficionados.

She punched numbers into the phone. "Mr. Welton? This is Carol Ashton. I'm returning your call."

"Inspector. Good. Need to see you immediately." He had a high, nasal voice and a snappy, irritated tone. "It's about Collis's suicide. Have information you might find interesting." Without waiting for a reply, he went on, "Be at the Con this afternoon, lecturing on composition. Could see you there about three. Suit you?"

Carol sat frowning after he had terminated their call. She remembered some story about an opera Welton was supposed to be working on—something to do with the infamous trial and conviction of Lindy Chamberlain, who claimed that her missing baby had

13

been carried off by a dingo. Welton certainly had written music specifically for Collis Raeburn, including a surprisingly melodic *Republic's Dawning* commissioned by a rich anti-monarchist and sung by Raeburn to a huge television audience tuned to watch the spectacular fireworks over Sydney on Australia Day last January.

How did Welton know so quickly that she had been put in charge of the case?

Shrugging, she turned to the post mortem report. Collis Raeburn, who had been rapidly attaining international superstardom, had been reduced by the State Morgue to a case number and a concise recital of facts. Everything about him seemed relentlessly average: height, weight, physical condition. His extraordinary talent, the glorious voice that had captivated so many people, had been diminished by the pathologist's scalpel to healthy vocal cords and a superior lung capacity. He had ingested, the report stated succinctly, amylobarbitone, pethidine and alcohol in sufficient quantities to cause his death, although what had actually killed him was suffocation, as, after he had slid into unconsciousness, he had choked on his own vomit. His stomach contained the partly digested remnants of a light meal. Time of death was difficult to establish, first, because it wasn't possible to determine exactly when he ate the meal, and second, because the air-conditioning in the room had been set on full, which affected rigor mortis. All things taken into consideration, the forensic pathologist was willing to set the parameters at somewhere between nine on Saturday night and one o'clock on Sunday morning.

She shuffled through the photographs taken at the scene, pausing over a close-up of Raeburn's long, sensitive fingers slightly curled as they brushed the thick carpet. The overturned tumbler glinted in the flash, the stain of spilled whiskey was faintly visible, scattered tablets fanned near his relaxed hand.

Mark Bourke put his head around the door. "Carol? Got something for you."

"Look at this photo, Mark. It looks staged to me."

"Raeburn was the theatrical type."

"You think he arranged the glass and the pills like this, then managed to fall unconscious with one hand draped artistically as part of the scene?"

Bourke sat down and stretched his long legs. "Just the way it happened. Takes *your* aesthetic eye, Carol, to see the artistry."

"And I don't like the fact there's no suicide note."

"Carol, there often isn't."

"It doesn't feel right. As you say, he was theatrical. It seems to me he'd have wanted the last word."

Bourke's smile was cynical. "Sure there wasn't a note, and it was embarrassing, so it's disappeared? Wouldn't be the first time a little judicious tampering occurs at the scene of a suicide."

"The two who discovered him didn't mention seeing a note." She handed him the preliminary report. "Have you read this?"

"Yes. To me it's classic suicide, and efficient, except he forgot to take the precaution of adding a nausea tablet to stop himself from vomiting. The nicely lethal combination of sleeping tablets, a narcotic and alcohol means he wasn't making a staged cry for help. He was deadly serious."

15

"There was a copy of *The Euthanasia Handbook* in the room."

He spread his hands. "Well, there you are, then. He has a textbook to check he's doing it right." He grinned wickedly. "Maybe the publishers can use it in their advertising—a famous satisfied customer's always good for business."

"It's too neat. I don't like it."

He shook his head. "If you're suggesting murder, you'll open an awfully restless can of worms. He was HIV-positive. That alone will galvanize the media if they get wind of it—and the longer his death's a news item, the more likely it is that someone will dig it up. Isn't your job to get this off the front pages as quickly as possible?"

"I'm not altogether sure what my job's supposed to be, Mark. What I do know is that there's some hidden agenda, and I'm going to find out what it is."

"You've got another complication. The word's around that Bannister, the guy you replaced on the case, isn't happy. Says it's political influence."

"It is."

"Yes, we all know that. But he's still bitching. Actually, I think he's put in an official complaint."

Impatient, Carol threw the photograph down. "The Commissioner appointed me because the Minister for Police told him to, so where's a complaint going to get Bannister?"

Bourke was smiling at her vehemence. "Calm down, Carol. Don't take it personally. I'd take it through channels too, if I were him. Just thought you should know that Bannister would be delighted to find something to hang a real complaint on, so watch your back."

"You're kidding me."

His smile faded. "No, I'm not. Bannister's new to the South Region, but I've had a bit to do with him over the years. He causes trouble, and none of the dirt clings to him. Efficient, ambitious and resentful. Probably the worst he could do is cause some aggravation, but it might be worth keeping an eye on him."

She began to twist her black opal ring. "I don't need this."

He cocked an eyebrow. "So, Carol, forgetting Bannister who's just an irritation, what's your professional opinion as opposed to your instinct? Is it suicide, murder or an unfortunate accident?"

"Probably suicide—but I was brought in for a purpose, and I don't think it's just because I'm supposed to be good at PR."

"Wanted someone with a higher profile than Bannister?"

"Could be. Which means the aim might be *more* publicity, not less. Why would that be, do you think?"

"Want me to do some digging?"

"Please. But be subtle, Mark."

His grin had returned. "Subtle," he said, "is my middle name."

After he had gone she read through the statements of the hotel staff and closely studied the photographs of the room. Collis Raeburn had checked into his usual luxury hotel near Circular Quay and had gone up to his room at 5:30 P.M. He'd unpacked his clothes and put them away, called room service and ordered an early meal and a bottle of wine. About nine he arranged for a large pot of coffee to

17

be left outside the door and had instructed the desk to not put through any calls to his room. The person who'd delivered the coffee to his floor remembered seeing the DO NOT DISTURB sign. He didn't knock, but left the coffee by the door. Several of the room photos showed the silver coffee pot and a cup and saucer sitting on a low table near easy chairs arranged at the window to take advantage of the beautiful view of Sydney Harbour.

Carol fanned out the photographs and considered them again. *Too neat. Too theatrical. And there should be a note.*

She frowned over a series of shots of the room, bed and body taken from different angles. Collis Raeburn was casually dressed: jeans, a loose cotton sweater and sports shoes. The investigating officer on the scene had noted that Raeburn had unpacked his suitcase and put his clothes away neatly, yet two of the photographs showed a necktie on the carpet near the foot of the bed, crumpled as though it had been carelessly tossed there.

In one extreme close-up of Collis Raeburn's face, his cheek was nestled deep into the comfort of a pillow, eyes closed, mouth slightly open. She remembered vividly the last time she had seen this dead face full of life: a television special hosted by the diminutive but formidable Madeline Shipley. The program traced his life and career, starting with his first singing experiences as a boy soprano in a church choir and interviewing important people in his life. Raeburn had sung some of his most famous arias, his mouth curved in a half-smile that his singing teacher, a pragmatic middle-aged woman, described clinically to the camera as, "Essential to

18

the production of a clear, forward tone." Popular far beyond opera circles, his voice caressed, warmed, captivated. And the joy with which he sang vitalized the most hackneyed song, the most familiar aria. Only in his early thirties, he was approaching his prime as a singer, his best years still ahead of him when his voice would mature and darken to suit the most demanding roles of grand opera.

Still staring at his face, she absently picked up the phone on its second ring. "Carol Ashton." She leaned back, smiling. "Darling, I'll be late too. I've been landed with the Collis Raeburn case. Let's get a pizza delivered when we both make it home."

As she replaced the receiver her imagination vividly held Sybil's red hair, the line of her jaw, the way her eyes crinkled when she laughed. But there were darker things—the note of impatience so often in Sybil's voice, the tension that had grown between them lately, the resentments that Carol tried to ignore.

She shrugged. She didn't want to think about that now.

CHAPTER TWO

The manager of the five-star hotel where Raeburn had died was a small, neat man with a pencil mustache and an affable, but restrained manner. He ushered Carol and Anne to seats, then retreated behind his mahogany desk. "Well, Inspector, we both know that now and then..." He paused delicately, "... a guest may take the unfortunate step of..."

"Suicide."

He seemed relieved the word was out. "Yes. And of course, we always cooperate fully with the authorities, whilst respecting the privacy of our guests."

"What procedures are followed when someone dies?"

"Generally we call for a doctor to be certain that the guest is ... deceased. There have been a few unfortunate cases where staff have reacted precipitately ..."

Carol saw Anne hide a smile. Recently there had been an embarrassing incident where hotel staff had found an international pop star apparently dead in his suite, and one enterprising member of the management had leaked this scoop to the media, unaware that the guest was in a deep drug-induced coma, but still very much alive. The resultant publicity and threats of legal action by the star had necessitated swift damage control by the hotel chain and had blighted career prospects for several members of staff.

"... then, of course, we contact the police and, where appropriate, the next of kin. You'll understand, Inspector, it's always a time where discretion is vital."

"I'd like a step-by-step outline of Collis Raeburn's stay, right through to the removal of the body." When the manager seemed about to protest, Carol added, "I'm quite aware you've been through this before, but I would appreciate it if you could outline it again."

The manager repressed a sigh. "Naturally, Inspector, we want to cooperate fully." He referred to notes in an embossed leather folder. "Let me see ... Mr. Raeburn checked in at five-thirty on Saturday, asking for his usual room with a view of the Opera

House and harbor. He arranged for room service to deliver a meal at seven-thirty." He looked up. "Are you interested in what he ate?"

"Of course."

"All he requested was a tuna salad and a bottle of white wine. No dessert, coffee only. I've spoken to the waiter who delivered the meal and he said that Mr. Raeburn seemed quite relaxed and happy."

"Yes. We have a statement from him."

The manager cleared his throat. "The last contact the hotel had with Mr. Raeburn was just after nine o'clock. He called to order a large pot of coffee, and also asked that no calls be put through to his room until further notice. The waiter—the same one who'd delivered the meal—saw the DND on the handle, and, naturally, didn't knock, but left the tray with the coffee outside the door."

"How long would a Do Not Disturb be honored?"

"Normally until after checkout time, which is noon, unless other arrangements have been made. If at this point the person didn't respond to a telephone call from the desk, a decision to enter the room would be made at the discretion of the Duty Manager. This didn't apply in the case of Mr. Raeburn because he was booked in for several days. What happened here was that the room attendants reported to the Housekeeping Supervisor that they couldn't enter the room to make the bed and change the towels. This was logged in the housekeeping department, and brought to the attention of the Duty Manager when the evening shift came on the next night."

"None of your staff had noticed any activity from the point where Raeburn ordered the coffee at nine?"

"Nothing. There were no calls in or out, no messages taken, and no one made any inquiries at the desk." He looked professionally regretful. "I'm afraid Mr. Raeburn was very careful not to be disturbed during his last hours."

"The tray with the remains of the tuna salad wasn't in the room. When would that have been collected?"

The manager gave a suggestion of a shrug. "Presumably Mr. Raeburn put it outside his room. Any staff involved in room service are instructed to clear trays immediately when they see them."

"We know the tray wasn't there when the coffee was left by the door."

A glimmer of impatience showed on the manager's face. "It may have been collected earlier, or later—there's no record kept of such things."

As Anne flipped a page of her notebook, Carol said, "Anyone could have gone to the room without checking in at the desk."

"Yes, of course. There's always movement in the lobby of a hotel. But the person would need to know the room number, otherwise he or she would ask at the desk and be told Mr. Raeburn was not to be disturbed."

"And no one did ask, according to your staff."

He raised his eyebrows fractionally. "They're reliable, and professional. If they say no one asked, no one did."

Carol said, "Collis Raeburn always had the same room?"

"Whenever possible. Do you want to see it, Inspector? We had permission from the detective in charge to clean the room, but we've booked no one into it . . ." He frowned. "Unfortunately we've had several requests to spend the night in the place where Mr. Raeburn died. It is not, of course, our policy to accede to such propositions."

"I'm sure it's not," said Carol, straight-faced. "I don't want to see the room, but I would like details about the discovery of the body."

"The night audit staff were on—they work through the night and do a printout of departures and stay-overs for the next day. The Housekeeping Supervisor was concerned about Mr. Raeburn and she approached the Duty Manager. Constant attempts during the evening had not elicited any reply from the room, so the Duty Manager spoke to the assistant manager and it was decided to open the door, in case Mr. Raeburn had been taken ill."

"Didn't your staff consider he'd gone out and forgotten to remove the sign from the door?"

"Mr. Raeburn *always* left the key at the desk, without exception, so it was obvious he was still in his room. And, of course, if he had gone out and for once forgotten to leave the key, no harm would have been done by entering his room."

"This is twenty-four hours since any contact with him?"

"Yes. Under other circumstances we might have done something sooner, but Mr. Raeburn was a regular guest and he liked his privacy, so staff were unwilling to impinge on that. When his body was discovered we immediately contacted the authorities."

"Did you ring his father or sister?"

"No. We left that to the police. My staff called me, of course, and I came in at once to handle any problems that might occur with the media."

"Were there any?"

The manager frowned thoughtfully. "At that point we'd contained the news. I did have one curious call, though . . ."

Carol felt a tingle of interest. "Why curious?"

"A very husky voice. Claimed to be a reporter with the *Sentinel*, and asked if it were true that Collis Raeburn had been found dead in his room."

"A man or a woman?"

His frown deepened. "Whoever it was just gave a surname. I thought it was a woman, but it could've been a man."

"Do you remember the name?"

Irritation flitted across his face. "I keep a record of all calls that are put through to me, especially at a time like this." He consulted a note. "The name was Oldfield, or something close to it. The voice wasn't very clear."

"How did you respond?"

"The standard reply—that it was hotel policy to make no comment of any sort on any guest. Whoever it was then broke the connection."

Carol glanced at Anne. "Check the name." She looked back at the manager. "So someone wanted to know if Collis Raeburn was dead, but you weren't any help. How was the body removed?"

The manager seemed offended at such bluntness. "We temporarily locked the guest elevators so they had to bypass the floor, then used the service elevator to take the body down to the loading dock at the back of the hotel."

"Would anyone be able to see the body being removed?"

Again an infinitesimal shrug. "It was done

25

discreetly early Monday morning, but I suppose someone could have been watching at some point." His voice became sententious as he added, "However, I want to emphasize, Inspector Ashton, that we saw it our duty to continue to extend to Mr. Raeburn in death the privacy he requested in life."

Carol asked when the staff who'd dealt with Raeburn on Saturday evening would be on duty again, and their names. "Sergeant Newsome may need to interview them briefly."

"Of course, Inspector," said the manager with the faintest of sighs.

As they got into the car in the hotel car park, Carol said to Anne, "Remember when you check out the *Sentinel* reporter who's supposed to have called, he or she may be a freelance using the paper's name for access. And I want you to contact the morgue and see if anyone rang them that morning about Raeburn. Someone was very anxious to be certain he was dead."

As she turned into the busy street, Anne said, "His death was hot news, so there must have been a scramble to get information as soon as something leaked."

"But that's the point, Anne. The report of the pop star's supposed death led to a couple of staff losing their jobs, so this time no one leaked anything. That means the person who called the manager knew ahead of time there was at least a possibility that Raeburn was dead."

Anne considered this for a moment, then said, "Maybe Raeburn *was* suicidal, and someone close to him realized he was very depressed. Could have been a friend checking up."

"An anonymous friend who claims to be a reporter?"

"People do odd things," said Anne, smiling.

"Raeburn's fingerprints were everywhere they should be, but if I were setting up a murder as suicide, I'd make sure of that anyway."

"But how would you get him to take all those tablets?"

"That," said Carol as they turned into Macquarie Street, "is where your creative imagination comes into play. Work out how you'd kill him, Anne, and while you're about it, come up with a stunning motive."

The Conservatorium of Music, affectionately known as the Con, sat in Macquarie Street at the edge of the splendid greenery of the Royal Botanic Gardens. A squat white building, modeled on the gatehouse of a Scottish castle, its turreted towers looked bizarre but appealing.

Carol and Anne Newsome were met at the entrance by Graeme Welton. He greeted them without enthusiasm, shaking hands briefly with Carol and nodding to Anne. His high voice and nasal twang seemed incongruous with his physical appearance. He was a bulky, thick-necked man with regular features and sparse mousy hair brushed forward, apparently to disguise his receding hairline.

"Thought I'd meet you at the door. Never find me otherwise." As he spoke, his fingers tugged at the lapels of his wine-red jacket, drifted across his face, pulled at an earlobe, smoothed his hair forward, finally coming to impatient rest in front of him, where he played, apparently unconsciously, elaborate finger games. Carol could see Anne staring at

Welton's hands; she herself inspected his face. He had ruddy skin, rather small but piercingly blue eyes, a wide, full-lipped mouth and a deep cleft in his chin.

"I'm a little surprised," said Carol, "that you knew I'd been put in charge of the case."

"Just heard it on the grapevine, Inspector."

It was obvious he wasn't going to elaborate. Carol said, "Is there somewhere we could go, Mr. Welton?"

"Yes, of course. It'll be cramped though. Practice room."

He led them at a fast pace, striding down the corridor with heavy steps. "In here. Your constable'll have to stand."

The cramped practice room was untidy with music manuscripts, angular metal sheet music stands and ill-matched furniture. Welton perched on a high stool, Carol folded herself onto an ancient low leather chair, Anne Newsome stood against the dingy wall, notebook and pen ready.

After gazing at Carol intently, he announced, "Well, Inspector, I'm impressed. You're even better looking than you are on television. Mind, I've always had a weakness for green-eyed blondes."

"Thank you. Now, you said on the phone you had information about Mr. Raeburn's death. When did you see him last?"

His response to her brisk tone was an unexpectedly charming smile. "So I've no hope of disarming you with compliments?"

"It's unlikely."

"Then I won't persevere, Inspector." He found a paper clip, and began to bend it out of shape. "Saw Collis on Friday afternoon. My place in Glebe."

When he didn't seem inclined to expand on this, Carol said, "At the end of this interview it would be helpful if you'd give Sergeant Newsome a detailed schedule of your movements from Friday to Monday."

"Don't tell me I need an alibi for Collis's suicide?" he exclaimed in mock horror. "Frankly, I don't have one." He shot a glance at Anne. "Note that I spent the weekend working alone, Constable."

"Noted," said Anne with the hint of a smile.

He turned back to Carol. "And Inspector, don't bother to say these questions are just routine. It's such a tired old line."

"Why did Mr. Raeburn come to your place on Friday?"

"We were discussing a current project of mine."

"*Dingo?*"

"Well, well! You have been doing your homework."

Ignoring his facetious tone, she said, "I've been told there was some conflict about your new opera. In fact, that Mr. Raeburn didn't want to sing in it."

Welton shrugged elaborately. "That's what comes from listening to gossip, Inspector. You don't get the story straight. It's true Collis had some initial concerns, but they'd all been ironed out, so no matter what anyone might tell you, there were no ongoing problems. He was contracted to sing the lead male role, and he was perfectly happy to be doing it."

Carol said, "Collis Raeburn was a friend as well as a colleague?"

"Yes. A close friend. We shared a great deal." The staccato rhythm of his voice slowed as he went on reflectively, "Music, of course. I wrote much of my work with Collis in mind. But we also enjoyed many of the same things—test cricket, bodysurfing, gourmet French food..."

"You said on the telephone that you had something of interest to tell me."

"Meaning that these musings aren't of interest? Or perhaps you have other important interviews this afternoon?" When Carol didn't respond, he went on, "Forgive me. I'm upset about Collis, of course. What I want to tell you concerns Edward Livingston. Know who he is?"

Carol gave a measured smile. "It would be difficult not to know, considering the amount of publicity he generates. I happened to be one of the many who watched the telecast of his production of *Nabucco* at the Sports Ground, complete with Jerusalem, the Hanging Gardens of Babylon and a cast of thousands."

Livingston was the controversial manager of the Eureka Opera Company. An Englishman, he'd been appointed over several qualified Australians vying for the position, and his abrasive manner and lack of reticence about his own abilities had ensured that his name was well-known even by people who had no interest in opera.

No one could ignore his productions. Either he was staging huge spectacles in outdoor sites, or taking popular operas and changing them, to traditionalists, in some shocking way. Carol remembered with amusement the stir he'd created a few months before by altering *Madame Butterfly* from a love story between a Japanese geisha and an American naval officer to an encounter between a call girl and an extraterrestrial. Simulcast with an

FM radio station, the live telecast had initially attracted huge ratings, but as the program went on, more and more viewers switched to other channels. Collis Raeburn had made a handsome, if somewhat unconvincing alien, while Butterfly had been sung by the prima donna of the Eureka Opera Company, Alanna Brooks.

"He drove Collis to his death."

It seemed he was waiting for some response to this statement. Eventually Anne looked up from her notes, and he said to her, "Suppose that sounds too dramatic, but it's true. Hounded him, never let him alone."

Carol said, "About what?"

Welton drummed his fingers against a rickety music stand. "About everything. Livingston was disappointed at his Pinkerton in *Madame Butterfly.* Said his acting wasn't up to scratch. Collis always had doubts about himself, no matter how successful he was. He didn't need criticism—he needed building up, trust, optimism. Livingston was bad for him."

"You must be aware suicide is one possibility." Carol waited for his acknowledging nod. "So are you suggesting Mr. Livingston's attitude would be enough to push Collis Raeburn to the point of killing himself?"

"No, no. Of course not. But it helped. Believe me, it helped." He smoothed his hair, tugged at his collar. "Livingston never let him alone. Always finding something to pick at, something to criticize."

"Why?"

"Why? The man can't help himself. Has to tear down anyone greater than himself. He was jealous of Collis. Of his fame, if you like."

31

"But surely Mr. Livingston's success depends on the talents of other artists. Isn't it to his advantage that they be famous?"

Welton tapped a fist against the palm of his other hand. "Secondary to him. It's all secondary to him. The artists, the music, the whole thing. *He* has to be first. Always him."

His bitterness hung in the air. Carol waited. He didn't continue. She said, "Do you have a personal grudge against Edward Livingston?"

He gave a snort of laughter. "Find someone who hasn't!"

Carol had decided to use Sykes and his professed public relations expertise after all: she had rerouted all calls from the media through him. When her phone rang she picked it up quickly, expecting the caller to be Sybil.

"Mum?"

"David! What a nice surprise." She could hear her voice becoming uncustomarily gentle. "Why are you ringing me at the office, darling?"

"About next weekend . . . Dad wants to talk to you."

She frowned as she listened to the mumbled conversation as her son handed the phone to Justin Hart.

"Carol? How are you?" Her ex-husband's loud, confident voice was as definite as he was in person. Without waiting for any response, he went on, "Look, sorry to do this with so little notice, but I've got a favor to ask. I'm going to a legal conference in

Melbourne this coming weekend and through to Tuesday, and at the last moment it looks like Eleanor can come with me, so I was wondering if you'd be able to take David. Say if you can't, of course. I realize you're on the Raeburn thing—saw you interviewed."

"I'd love to. Anyway, Aunt Sarah's coming down from the Blue Mountains tomorrow night for a week, and she'll be staying with us, so it'll work out well."

"Fine," he said heartily. "Drop David over Saturday morning, then. That okay?"

Carol was smiling with the delight of having David to herself for several days. "I'll pick him up from your place, if you like."

"No, Carol. We'll be on the way to the airport, so it won't be any trouble. Hold on a moment..." She heard him say to David, "Go tell Eleanor it's okay with Carol." Back on the line, he said with a change of tone, "We do need to talk, sometime soon."

She took a deep breath, suspecting what he was about to say. "What about?"

"About you. He has to know, Carol. And you have to be the one to tell him."

She shut her eyes. "All right, Justin. After you get back, we'll talk."

His voice was again full of forceful certainty. "Great. Well, thanks for being so helpful. See you Saturday."

Before she could ask to speak to David again, he'd broken the connection. She sat looking at the phone. What could she tell her ten-year-old son that he would understand?

* * * * *

As Carol was packing her briefcase, preparatory to a late departure for home, Anne Newsome came into her office. "No one named Oldfield works for the *Sentinel,* either permanently, or freelance. The closest names they could come up with are Oakley or Bradfield, but neither reporter had anything to do with the Raeburn story."

"And the morgue?"

"Couldn't get anything out of them. Of course their policy is to give no information to the public, so it's not surprising that no one remembers a call from an Oldfield."

Carol snapped her briefcase shut. "Some reporters would have an inside working relationship with staff at the morgue—it's the way things work. When you get a spare minute follow it up, but it's not urgent, okay?"

As she drove across the Harbour Bridge, mind in neutral, a conviction swam up into her consciousness. She felt a sudden thrill, as though she'd caught a glimpse of her quarry. *Someone killed you. Cold-bloodedly. Carefully. And I'll find out who . . .*

CHAPTER THREE

Over breakfast, Sybil handed her a stiff rectangular card. "Forgot to show you this last night. It came addressed to both of us, so I opened it."

The embossed invitation requested the company of Carol Ashton and Sybil Quade at the wedding of Patricia James and Marcus Bourke at Balmoral Beach and afterwards at the Bathers Pavilion Restaurant at the same location. Carol smiled at the "Marcus," wondering why Mark had let it through.

"Carol? We're going?"

Don't push it. Carol looked at the familiar lines

of Sybil's slim figure, the dusting of freckles across her nose, her direct, frank gaze, and felt a rush of anger. "Mark's my friend. He wouldn't understand if I didn't go."

"That's not what I mean. We've been asked together."

Carol flicked the card onto the kitchen bench. "Pat knows we live in the same house. It'd be stupid to send separate invitations."

"Carol . . ."

Slamming her open palm on the bench top, Carol said, "As far as I'm concerned, we're not going *together*—we're going at the same time."

"Why?"

"You know why. Colleagues, superiors will be there. To all intents it'll be a police wedding."

"And you can't be seen with me."

"Not the way you want to be. I can't do it, Sybil. You don't understand. It'd stuff my career if I was openly a lesbian."

Sybil was as bitterly angry as Carol. "What do you think I'm going to do? Wear overalls and a Lesbian Nation T-shirt? Kiss every woman in sight passionately? Wave a placard telling everyone we're lovers?"

"Stop trying to manipulate me!"

"Manipulate you? I wouldn't know how to begin. You're set like concrete, Carol. You won't even listen, will you?"

"Give me a break!"

A pause, then Sybil said quietly, "This is too important to be yelling about. We should talk about it."

"No."

"No?"

"I'm sick of talking. You know what the situation is as far as my work's concerned. Outside that, okay. But this wedding is *work,* Sybil."

"So that's it?"

To herself, Carol's voice sounded cold and final. "That's it."

"Murder?" repeated the Commissioner, heavy brows frowning. "I've seen Bannister's initial report. Don't see where you get that scenario, and I certainly don't want it mentioned in the press meeting we're having this morning."

The Commissioner hadn't offered her a seat. Carol put her hands into the jacket pockets of her navy blue suit. "I thought you should know I think it's a possibility."

He grunted, surveyed her soberly. "There's going to be a State funeral for Raeburn next week. Are you going to hold up release of the body?"

"That shouldn't be necessary."

"Homicide will complicate things."

"Yes, I know."

He smiled briefly. "Warned the Minister you'd run it your way. Told her if she wanted someone amenable, there were others who'd be a better bet." He stood, indicating the meeting was over. "Do what you have to do, but keep me informed every step of the way. I don't want any surprises."

"There's something else . . ."

"Important?"

"Very. Collis Raeburn was HIV-positive. If during

the interviews it becomes obvious that the person's had unprotected sex—"

"You say nothing," he interrupted. "The lid's got to be on this, at least at the moment."

"What if someone unknowingly infects another person?" Carol asked, her anger evident.

"All right, I see your point. You can advise the appropriate health authorities and let them deal with direct notification, if necessary. I don't want AIDS or HIV linked to the investigation in any way, so neither you nor any of your team are to warn anybody. Is that clear?"

As she reached the door, he added, "I'll see you at ten for the press conference... And Carol, I'm willing to back you on this case, but be careful. We're talking a lot of politics here."

Simon Sykes hovered anxiously around Carol and the Commissioner as the microphones were set up. "I'd be the last to advise you, Carol, but this is a delicate situation, and the Minister will be watching..."

Carol fixed him with the coldest look she could muster. "Go away," she said. He went.

Under the warmth of the television lights and to the accompaniment of clicking shutters from the press photographers, Carol went through her paces. Yes, she was in charge of the investigation of Collis Raeburn's death. No, she was unable to comment in detail because she was new to the case. The fact that she'd replaced Detective Sergeant Bannister was an administrative decision which was outside her area. No, she couldn't comment on the possibility of suicide—her team was making a full investigation.

She parried questions on the Raeburn family's response to the tragedy; whether or not she was an opera fan; if there was any possibility of foul play; had Collis Raeburn left a note; did rivalry in the singing world have anything to do with his death; the predictable rumor that he had had throat cancer and was facing a silent future; did she have a personal opinion, or even a hunch, regarding his death . . .

Afterwards, the Commissioner's comment was a sardonic accolade. "Vintage Inspector Ashton," he said. "You charmed the pants off them, Carol, but told them buggerall."

Anne Newsome drove with her usual competence to the Raeburn estate at Galston, Carol beside her. As they entered the more rural areas of Sydney's north, the vitality of early spring became obvious. Everything was washed with a green, glowing patina, and to Carol the feeling of renewal was exhilarating.

She glanced at the young constable beside her. "Anne, you've read through everything on Collis Raeburn's death, haven't you?"

"Yes." A grin. "Why do I feel you're about to ask me something I can't answer?"

"Describe the possible scenarios, as you see them."

Her eyes on the road, Anne said, "His death looks like suicide, and if Mr. Raeburn hadn't been so famous, I imagine that wouldn't have ever been questioned."

Carol leaned back and relaxed. She felt the pleasure of a teacher with a promising student. "Go on."

"Okay. He finds out he's HIV-positive and he can't face what that will mean. Besides that, he's never formed a permanent relationship with anyone, so it's possible he feels alienated and lonely anyway. He decides to kill himself. There's been plenty of publicity about *The Euthanasia Handbook* so he buys a copy to get reliable information. He discovers he already has the necessary drugs, puts the pills in his luggage, buys a bottle of Johnny Walker, and checks himself into his favorite hotel. He has a last meal, orders coffee, stops any telephone calls and puts a Do Not Disturb on the door. He takes a handful of pills, drinks whiskey and falls unconscious on the bed. Before he can die of the combination of drugs and alcohol, he vomits while unconscious, and chokes. He wouldn't know anything about it and the effect is the same. He's dead."

Carol waited while Anne overtook a lumbering truck, then said, "Why didn't he leave a note?"

After considering the question, Anne said, "I'm not sure, but lots of people who suicide don't leave notes. Perhaps he couldn't be bothered, or he didn't need to justify himself." She had a sudden thought that obviously pleased her. "I know—he was killing himself for himself, if you see what I mean. He didn't want to have revenge on anybody, or make them feel guilty, so there wasn't any reason to leave a note behind."

"Interesting thought," said Carol, amused at Anne's delight at her own hypothesis. "Now, what if it happened to be an accident, as Raeburn's father and sister are insisting?"

Anne said immediately, "It would be the best possible scenario as far as most people are concerned. Just as a matter of course, Raeburn takes his sleeping tablets and painkillers along to the hotel with him. He's feeling a bit low, so he buys a bottle of whiskey to drown his sorrows. He wants to be left alone, so he stops his calls and makes sure no one will knock on the door. His back's hurting, he wants a good night's sleep, so he takes some pills, but he's been drinking steadily, first wine with his meal, and then whiskey, so he gets confused. Maybe he dozes off and wakes up again. Can't remember what he's taken, so he has some more. Unfortunately, the combination's fatal, and he dies, like before."

"Why does he have the television on so loudly?"

Anne glanced at her. "I don't understand. Why not?"

"You say he's tired and he wants to go to sleep. So why have the volume up so high? Why have it on at all?"

The sign indicating the Galston turnoff loomed on the right. Anne braked suddenly and turned at the intersection. Abashed, she said, "Sorry, I didn't realize we were so close to the turn."

You so remind me of myself at your age ... wanting to impress by doing everything well. Carol said, "The television?"

"Maybe he meant to turn it off, but never got round to it."

As they sped past a row of shops sitting in lonely isolation along the edge of a paddock, Carol said, "Do you have a third scenario?"

"Yes. Murder."

"You almost sound pleased with the idea."

Anne gave her a quick glance. "I'm not pleased, but if it *is* murder, it's someone being very clever..."

Carol knew what she meant. "Matching wits, is that what you mean?"

Anne nodded. "I've imagined how I'd do it..."

"How?"

"All right, first I've got to have a motive strong enough to make me want to kill him. Sometime after he has his meal delivered, I go straight up to his room. I don't ask at the desk because I know the number. He lets me in. Either I know he's got the narcotics and painkillers with him, or I've brought them along with me. I might also have brought the bottle of whiskey. We talk, he orders a pot of coffee, I get him to take the tablets somehow or other. He's drunk, confused. I feed him more drugs. When he's unconscious, I turn the television volume up and leave. Sometime in the next hour or so he dies, and I'm well away from the place."

She slowed down to turn onto a narrow road that was sign-posted with the name Raeburn, a statement that it was a private road and a threat that trespassers would be prosecuted. Carol said to her, "How can you be certain he's going to die?"

Anne bit her lip. "Oh, God. Imagine staying there in the room, waiting... I couldn't do it."

"Maybe you could, if you hated him enough."

An ornate sign declared grandly RAEBURN

ESTATE. Set on several acres in the semi-rural area, the house was a two-story red-brick building with no character, no style. It sat morosely in a blank expanse of mowed lawn dotted with a few scraggly shrubs.

"It looks," said Anne, "like it's been picked up from a conservative suburb and plopped down here in the middle of a paddock."

As they went to the front door Carol had to agree that this expensive house looked uncomfortably out of place, and totally alien to the environment in which it found itself.

The Raeburns' housekeeper, Martha, was a barrel-shaped woman. "Inspector Ashton," she said authoritatively when she opened the door, "I'm Martha Brownlye, the housekeeper. You look just like your photographs." Before Carol could speak, she went on, "The family's so pleased you're looking after the case. And I am, too, of course. I've been with the Raeburns for thirty-five or more years, since just before Mrs. Raeburn died."

Carol, murmuring the appropriate response, wondered in amusement if the woman would suddenly present her with a printed curriculum vitae and references. As they were ushered in, Carol said, "Ms Brownlye, I'd like to see you before I go. Would that be possible?"

Obviously flattered, Martha nodded, then resumed her monologue. "And the tragedy has broken the family. It'll never be the same. I don't know what's to become of this house, for instance. It was built as a retreat for Collis, you see. It's really a bit too far out from town, but it was essential for him to get away from the pressures. There's a practice room, of course, and his voice coach came out here regularly—"

She stopped abruptly as a man appeared at the bottom of the hall. "Thank you, Martha," he said softly, but with an emphasis that sent her hurrying off to the back of the house.

Carol's first impression of Kenneth Raeburn was that he was a bantam rooster of a man. Shorter than Carol, he wore a dark suit and a burgundy bow tie and stood defiantly tall, his chin out-thrust, shoulders back, arms slightly bent and close by his body, giving Carol the impression that his heels were lifted so that he was poised on his toes. His iron-gray hair was still thick, and styled, she thought fleetingly, to add to his height. He had a hollow-cheeked, ascetic face, deepset eyes accented by heavy dark eyebrows and a nose that looked as though it had received severe punishment. His aura of pugnacity made Carol suspect that perhaps he'd been a boxer, who'd made up for his lack of height with ferocity.

He gravely shook hands with both Carol and Anne, then ushered them into a lounge room. The furniture had the same dissonance as the house, belonging, as did the house, to another kind of surroundings altogether. The spare lines and bright fluorescent green of the Swedish-style couch, chairs and low table did not suit the regency stripe curtains nor the elaborate embossed wallpaper and flowered carpet. A rosewood grandfather clock stood heavily in one corner.

Anne Newsome positioned herself at the other

end of the couch, Raeburn sat opposite Carol. "Coffee? Tea?"

"Thank you, but no."

"Inspector Ashton," he said slowly. His voice was disconcertingly soft, and Carol had to resist the urge to lean forward to hear him clearly. Apparently waiting to ensure he had their complete attention, he paused until Anne Newsome had opened her notebook and looked up expectantly.

"I've been told you're the best the Commissioner can offer me."

Carol thought, *You're a controller.*

Raeburn was watching her closely. Almost in a whisper, he said, "Collis died because of a dreadful accident. He was taking painkillers and sleeping tablets—he had a bad back, I suppose you know that—and he became confused, took too many, drank too much whiskey."

Aware that her voice sounded loud next to his quiet tones, she said, "I'm preparing a report for the coroner, Mr. Raeburn, and I must tell you that the evidence seems to indicate at least the possibility of suicide."

"No." His soft voice was not emphatic, but very sure. "Suicide is impossible. Completely impossible."

"He usually stayed at a hotel in the city when he had rehearsals or a performance?"

"Always. Collis found it too tiring to drive from here, so there was nothing at all unusual about that, Inspector."

"Your son called the hotel desk about nine o'clock and was very emphatic that no phone calls be put through and that he not be disturbed for any reason at all."

"So? That only means he didn't want to be interrupted."

"You were here? He didn't call you?"

A look of pain crossed Kenneth Raeburn's face. "I was here most of the time, but Collis didn't telephone."

"There was a copy of *The Euthanasia Handbook* in the room."

"Yes?" An irritated click of his tongue. "Every second person's bought a copy, it seems to me. The Handford action made sure of that. Collis was interested in the case itself."

He was referring to a case currently before the courts. A university lecturer, diagnosed with early Alzheimer's disease, had used a suicide method detailed in the handbook—tranquilizers and a plastic bag over the head—to successfully kill herself. The Handford family were in the process of suing both the publisher and the author for substantial damages, holding *The Euthanasia Handbook* wholly responsible for the death of their beloved family member.

For the first time Raeburn broke eye contact. He glanced at the constable, who was studiously writing, then said jerkily, "Inspector, you haven't mentioned murder. I don't for one moment believe that Collis was murdered, but are you considering it?"

Intrigued by his agitation, she said evenly, "It's one possibility."

"I can't imagine anyone would want to kill Collis. He was respected, loved. His death is a grievous blow, not only to Nicole and myself, but to everyone who treasured his voice."

That sounds like a set piece you've carefully rehearsed. "Nevertheless, there are some people who seemed to have grudges against your son."

"Indeed?" His voice was suddenly louder. "I imagine, if that's so, that Welton and Livingston are the two you have in mind."

"Why do you say that?"

He frowned impatiently. "I presume you do your job competently, Inspector. Then you would know that Graeme Welton has written an opera that is set to be an unmitigated disaster." A corner of his mouth lifted. "*Dingo,* I believe it's called," he said scathingly. "It was specifically written for Collis and Alanna Brooks, and the two of them were incautious enough to sign undertakings to take part in the premiere. I can assure you that when they realized the quality, or lack of it, they both were reluctant to be involved."

Carol decided that this was a good time to use some interesting items Anne Newsome had turned up in her investigation of the complicated web of Raeburn family finances. She said, "And you were involved, as well."

"What?"

"I've been advised you invested in the forthcoming opera. Was it on your own behalf?"

His eyes narrowed at her question. "I was Collis's manager," he ground out. "I handled all the financial aspects—investments, property purchases, and the like. It was perfectly normal to put money into a project he'd be singing in."

It was almost a pleasure to needle him. "You said yourself you thought it likely to be a disaster. Did you mean artistically, or financially?"

He moved impatiently. "Both. I'm not trying to hide the fact I had poor judgment in this case, but I put the money in before I realized what a turkey *Dingo* was going to be."

"You expect to lose your entire investment?"

"Very possibly. I can't get it out, as Welton had his accountants tie it up."

"Did your son resent that?"

Raeburn ducked his head, and suddenly his softer voice was almost inaudible. "Doubt if he even knew we had money invested there. Collis wasn't interested in the financial side of things. Details bored him. That's why I handled the money, and Nicole looked after all the bookings, the tour arrangements, etcetera."

"Did he agree with you that the opera was unlikely to be a success?"

This question elicited an unexpected response. Raeburn became animated, his voice becoming louder as he said, "Agree? He was the one who told me. Said he'd seen the libretto and the music, and it was amateurish, embarrassingly bad. Collis had it out with Welton. Said he wouldn't ruin his reputation singing such rubbish. They fought over it, because Collis had signed a contract to sing the premiere, and Welton was holding him to it."

He paused, seeming to realize he was talking too loudly, and brought his voice back to its customary softness. "I'd decided we had to break the contract. I had the lawyers working on it when Collis died."

There's something here . . . "Graeme Welton says

48

he had a meeting with your son on Friday, and everything was smoothed over. You didn't know anything about this?"

He glared at her. "Collis would have told me if that had happened, and he didn't. That makes Welton a liar." He added quickly, "Don't misunderstand, Inspector. I should have said that Graeme Welton's made a *mistake*. He's a friend of my daughter's, and I suppose he wanted to have the conflict resolved for her sake, so he saw this discussion with Collis in a much rosier light than it deserved."

In the silence the faint sound of Anne's pen seemed to remind him that his words were being recorded. He looked over at her, then back to Carol. She delayed until he fidgeted uncomfortably, then she said, "And Edward Livingston? You mentioned him as having a grudge against your son . . ."

"Livingston's impossible. Sooner or later everyone finds that out. Collis didn't like him. Livingston has no idea how to handle artists. Big, splashy productions are his style. No aesthetic taste, but he gets to the masses."

"This makes Mr. Livingston an asset to Eureka Opera?"

He frowned impatiently. "If you're talking dollars, Inspector, then *yes*, he is valuable to the Company. If you're referring to aesthetics, to artistic direction . . . well . . ."

"Was there some specific conflict between your son and Mr. Livingston?"

Again he clicked his tongue irritably. "It was Welton's bloody opera again. It was bad enough that it was unsingable, but on top of that, Livingston's planning to stage it in his usual ludicrous way. Ayers Rock on stage, trained dingoes and kangaroos..." His face was twisted with bitter amusement. "Can you imagine it, Inspector? An artist like Collis singing arias in the middle of a zoo? The whole idea was ridiculous, farcical." He stood up and began to stride around the room. "I would not permit Collis to be associated with such a production."

"But," said Carol mildly, "he would have had to sing in it, if his contract couldn't be broken. Isn't that so?"

Raeburn was checking his watch. "Inspector, I'm so sorry," he said smoothly, his agitation abruptly under control. "I have an urgent appointment. My daughter, however, is very keen to see you. I'll have to leave, I'm afraid, but Martha will look after you."

"There is one important matter..."

He said curtly, "Yes? What?"

Carol said with deliberate bluntness, "Your son was HIV-positive."

"I don't have time to discuss this now."

You don't have time to discuss that your son had the AIDS virus? "I'm sorry, but we do need to talk about it."

He was already at the door. He turned back to say harshly, "First, I don't accept that Collis had... the virus. It was a mistake with the blood test, or whatever. Second, I'll take legal action against anyone..." He paused for emphasis, "... *anyone* mentioning HIV-positive and my son's name in the same sentence." Again he reminded Carol of a bantam rooster swollen with arrogant authority. "I'll instruct Martha to get Nicole for you."

50

Carol stood. "Before you go, Mr. Raeburn, would you mind if we took a look at your son's room?"

"Your people have already been through his papers."

Carol nodded, but remained silent. *You like calling the shots and you don't want to accede to any request I make.*

After a moment he said impatiently, "All right. I can't see any harm in it."

The heavy tick of the grandfather clock seemed much louder after he had gone. Carol was able only to exchange a glance with Anne Newsome before Martha appeared with a tray which she set down at the central coffee table. "Thought you'd want refreshments. He's so upset. Did you realize that? The funeral, too, it'll be a dreadful ordeal. They say there'll be thousands there. Will you be going?"

Before Carol could respond, a woman came into the room. "Thanks, Martha. I'll look after everything."

As Carol stood, she noticed Nicole Raeburn's extreme slimness. Her wrists and ankles seemed to be fragile, breakable joints, her neck too thin to support her head with its abundance of chestnut hair.

Carol shook hands, the bony fingers barely brushing hers before being withdrawn. *Anorexic?* she thought, considering the narrow shoulders and concave chest. *Or sick? Asthma, maybe?*

When it became obvious that Nicole Raeburn was going to sit beside Carol on the sofa, Anne Newsome rose unobtrusively and went to a chair. Carol waited until she was settled, then said, "Of course you've been interviewed before, and I'm afraid I'll be asking the same questions you've already answered."

"It's no trouble. Besides, I was the one who suggested to Daddy that he get you put in charge."

Carol noted the childishness of the "Daddy," the breathless little-girl delivery, and the shrewd look behind the manner.

"Kind of you to suggest me."

Carol's dry tone won a beguiling smile. "You're annoyed with me, I know it. But the Minister of Police—Auntie Marge—she's not really an aunt, but she's such a good friend. You don't blame me for pulling a few strings, do you?"

What would you say if I asked why you and your father should expect special concessions? thought Carol. She said, "What can you tell me about your brother that would help me?"

Nicole Raeburn's eyes filled with tears. "My brother . . ." she whispered.

"I'm sorry it's necessary to intrude at such a time," said Carol, cynically aware of how many occasions she had said these words by rote.

"It's all right, really it is. Just so we can get everything straightened out. So no one will think that Colly killed himself." For a moment she rested a thin hand on Carol's arm. "It had to be an accident. He'd never do that. Colly had so much to live for . . ." Her voice strengthened. "And he never would have gone that way, without leaving a letter to me. We were so close. More than just brother and sister."

Carol found herself raising a mental eyebrow. Surely Nicole Raeburn wasn't hinting at incest?

Apparently the same interpretation had occurred

to Nicole. "I mean," she said hastily, "we were *companions, friends.* We shared everything. Personally. Professionally. If we didn't see each other, we spoke every day on the phone, no matter where he was—interstate, in another country, anywhere."

"He slept here, at home, on Friday?"

"Yes, but he had rehearsals and things for *Aida,* so he said he'd check into the hotel from Saturday onwards."

"Did he contact you after he left on Saturday morning?"

Clearly she wanted Carol to believe she would have been astonished if her brother hadn't called. "Oh, yes, of course he did. Quite early in the evening after he'd checked in."

"Did he seem upset?"

"No, he was just as usual. That's why I'm sure it was an accident, a stupid, pointless accident."

"He wasn't slurring his words, or anything like that?" At Nicole's frown, she added, "I'm trying to establish when he first might have been affected by the drugs or alcohol."

Lips trembling, she said, "He was my Colly just like he always was."

"And you were here, at home, Saturday and Sunday?"

Nicole looked at her knowingly. "You're asking that for a reason, aren't you?"

Carol sighed to herself. "It's a routine question," she said pleasantly. "Were you here?"

"Yes I was. And so was Daddy." There was calculation in her wide-eyed stare. "You're thinking someone wanted to hurt Colly?"

"Can you think of anyone who might wish him harm?"

Even though Carol had spoken in a mild tone, Nicole reacted with dramatic urgency. Her thin fingers closing around Carol's wrist, she exclaimed, "Murder? You're not thinking of murder? You're not thinking of that?" She released her, put a hand to her mouth. "Murder . . ."

Extraordinary. She likes the idea.

Nicole grew purposefully calm, twisting a strand of thick chestnut hair around her fingers as she said, "There *were* some people who were jealous of Colly."

"Any obvious conflicts?"

"Well, there's Livvy. You must know about him."

"Edward Livingston?"

"Yes. But he fights with everyone. And his stupid *Madame Butterfly* wasn't as successful as he hoped, so he blamed Colly, when it was absolutely obvious Alanna Brooks was the one not up to standard."

As Carol noted that Alanna Brooks didn't rate a diminutive, Nicole went on, "And Lloyd Clancy hated Colly because he knew it was only a matter of time before Colly eclipsed him totally. I mean, he was all right as a tenor, but next to my brother's voice . . . lead next to gold."

The way she said the last phrase convinced Carol that she was quoting someone else. "How about Graeme Welton?"

Nicole smiled, a brilliant rectangular smile that stretched the skin of her face and suggested to Carol the skull beneath. "Welty! He *loved* Colly. He loves us all. He's just one of the family."

"I've heard there's a problem with the opera he's written for Alanna Brooks and your brother."

"*Dingo?* It's the name, Inspector. It sounds awful, doesn't it? But I've seen the score and it's beautiful music."

"You're musical yourself?"

Nicole glanced down modestly. "Violin. Perhaps I could've pursued a concert career..." Left unsaid were the words: But I sacrificed it all for my brother.

"Did you happen to mention to Graeme Welton that I was in charge of the case?"

Nicole pouted slightly. "Yes I did. Was that wrong of me, Inspector?"

"Of course not. I just wondered when he contacted me how he had found out that I'd been put in charge."

"Oh, I tell him everything. Next to Colly, he's my best friend."

"Would your brother have told Mr. Welton about his blood test?"

Nicole Raeburn balked at the question. "Don't know what you mean." She sank back into the couch, turning her head away.

Carol kept her voice bland. "I'm sorry. I understood that you'd been told..."

"Colly didn't have AIDS!"

Anne shifted slightly at the agitation in Nicole Raeburn's voice. Carol said, "We know his doctor arranged the blood test for insurance purposes. It was totally unexpected when the results showed he was HIV-positive, and his doctor told him face-to-face and arranged for counseling."

Her stubborn certainty snapping her upright, she stared challengingly at Carol. "The whole thing is a mistake. Anything else is impossible." When Carol

55

didn't respond, she added with intensity, "And I expect you'll prove that, if you do your job properly."

Martha opened the door to Collis Raeburn's bedroom with a reverent expression, her voice hushed as she said, "Everything's as he left it. I tidied up after your police officers had finished going through his things, that's all." She paused irresolutely, then added, "I'll leave you to it, then . . ."

The room was luxuriously appointed. The bedroom was a generous size and off it ran a dressing room, each wall a mirror, and a black-tiled bathroom with a sunken tub. The carpet was pale beige, the bedspread and upholstered chairs a matching, but deeper, shade. The French windows opened out to a small balcony over which eucalyptus gums crowded. A massive rolltop desk sat solidly in one corner. The walls of the bedroom were covered with framed photographs, opera posters, brochures and programs, all jostling each other for space. Collis Raeburn, dressed in a series of magnificent costumes, stared majestically from frame after frame, only occasionally sharing the space with another person. Carol recognized Graeme Welton in several, solemnly staring at the camera. On a wall apart from the rest was a little island of family photographs showing Raeburn at various ages from early childhood. Carol noticed that he was always in the front, always striking a pose.

"That's Alanna Brooks," said Anne as she indicated a publicity shot for *La Boheme* with

Rodolfo and Mimi locked in an embrace that took care to give them enough room to allow their voices to soar together in a love duet. She surprised Carol by adding, "I saw that production. It was the first opera I ever went to ... my Dad used to sing himself—not opera, though—and he likes that sort of thing, so he took me."

"Did you enjoy it?"

Anne made a face, as though opera was something she felt obliged to reject. "I did, sort of ... I mean, it was romantic and dramatic and had a sad ending. Bit like a soap on TV, but with everyone singing their lines."

Carol was curious. "What did you think of Collis Raeburn? Did he make an impression on you?"

"He was wonderful," she said simply. "Everything became electric when he was on stage, and even I could tell his voice was something special."

Carol looked at the crowded walls. Frozen there were triumphs, but the man who had had an incomparable, thrilling voice had apparently locked himself away in the anonymity of a hotel room and taken his own life. "I don't believe he killed himself," she said.

Anne, alert but silent, waited. At last she said, "If it wasn't an accident, who murdered him?"

Carol gestured at the jam-packed photographs. "Someone up there," she said.

Martha welcomed them into the kitchen, which, like the rest of the house, combined disparate styles. There was a heavy scoured table, obviously antique, a scattering of polished copper pans on one wall, modern cupboards in pale wood and black metal chairs that proved to be as uncomfortable as they looked. Unasked, Martha slapped mugs of coffee in front of them. "Don't drink it if you don't want it."

Without preliminary fencing, Carol said, "Do you know any reason why Collis Raeburn should kill himself?"

"He wouldn't. It had to be an accident."

"He took sleeping tablets regularly?"

"Had trouble sleeping. He did his back in when he had a bad fall in *Tosca* last year. Constant, nagging pain, but he didn't want anyone to know. I don't know if you're aware of this, Inspector, but an opera singer has to be fit. Not just the voice, but the whole body. Until the accident he worked out every day—there's a gym room here—swam laps at North Sydney Pool twice a week for breath control, and watched his health. Lately, he'd been putting on weight, and that worried him."

"He was on a diet?"

"I told him—salads. He complained it was rabbit food, but he always listened to me. Always brought his problems to me." A spasm of grief washed across her face. "I've known him since he was a little boy. That's how I know he didn't kill himself."

"He confided in you..." Carol let her voice trail off to entice a response, but was still surprised at the frankness of Martha's response.

"You mean about the HIV? Yes, he told me. He knew I'd never repeat it, and he was absolutely devastated. He had no idea, you see. It was a blood test for an insurance policy, and when the results came in and the doctor told him, he came home to me and he cried."

How would I tell something so terrible to people I loved? "Did he tell his father and sister?"

"I don't know. *I* certainly didn't discuss it with them."

Phrasing her next question was a problem. "Did he say—"

"How he got it?" Martha interrupted. "No. I supposed it was drugs—sharing a needle."

"You know for a fact he took drugs?" asked Carol. The autopsy report had indicated there were no needle marks on the body. She made a mental note to follow up on the blood tests.

Martha's tone was indulgent. "Mr. Collis was a high-flier. He moved in circles where cocaine and such like are commonplace."

"So he definitely used drugs?"

"I didn't say that! I just said he might have used them. How else could he have contracted the virus?" To Carol's silence, she said sharply, "He wasn't queer, if that's what you think."

"He wouldn't have to be," said Carol flatly. "Was he going out with anyone in particular?"

Martha shook her head. "No. He played the field, when he had the opportunity. You must remember, Inspector, singing was his life and it took all his time and energy. There wasn't much room for anything else."

Thinking of the deadly virus he had unwittingly carried, Carol said, "You can't name any specific romantic interest?"

"He's always had a soft spot for Alanna Brooks. I

like her and I used to hope they'd get together, but nothing ever came of it. Lately he's supposed to be having a relationship with that young one, Corinne Jawalski, but that was all gossip. He never brought her home here, anyway." Her smile had a slightly malicious tinge as she added, "Not that he'd have wanted to, with his sister the way she is . . ."

Raising her eyebrows didn't elicit anything further, so Carol prompted, "The way she is . . ."

"Possessive," said Martha. "They're a close family—a very close family."

"Outsiders might not be welcome?"

Carol had gone too far. Martha's face closed. "I didn't say that."

"Were you here during the weekend?"

"No. I had Saturday and Sunday off. Went to stay with my sister at Bondi Beach. Mr. Collis gave me a lift into the city and I caught a bus out to the beach."

"Can you remember what he was wearing?"

The housekeeper looked at her with surprise. "What he was wearing? Something casual—jeans and some sort of white top, I think."

"Looking back now, can you remember anything that might have indicated he was thinking about killing himself?"

Her eyes suddenly overflowing, Martha said, "He would have said something to me if he was going to do that. He'd know I'd understand. We'd talked about how he felt he had a death sentence hanging over him, but he was determined to fight it." She anticipated Carol's next question. "No, he wasn't so depressed that he'd do something drastic. He *wasn't*."

She took out a handkerchief and blew her nose noisily. "Sorry. I get a bit emotional."

"One thing," said Carol, watching her closely, "that may point to his death being accidental is that he didn't leave a note in the hotel room." She paused, then said in a tone of polite inquiry, "Don't suppose he left anything here?"

Martha lifted her chin. "You think he left a suicide note here? Your people went through all his papers. If there was one, they would have found it."

"If it was still there," said Carol mildly.

Indignation struggled with grief on the housekeeper's face. "You believe I'd destroy a note, do you? Why would I do that?"

"To protect the family . . . Collis Raeburn's name . . . any number of reasons."

She blew her nose a final time, then faced Carol resolutely. "There wasn't anything. No note—nothing. He kept a journal, wrote in it most days. If he was going to say anything, it would have been in that."

"Where is this journal?"

"Your people must have taken it, I couldn't find it when I looked."

"Why were you looking for the journal?"

Offended, Martha said, "Nicole asked me to . . . I wasn't snooping, if that's what you mean."

"It was kept in the rolltop desk in his bedroom?"

"Yes, with his other papers." She gave a sad smile. "It was bound in black leather with his name in gold lettering, a present from Nicole a couple of years ago. You know, Inspector, Collis was always collecting photos, articles, reviews, programs, all the time. I used to cut things out of papers, save them for him. Said it would make it easier for his biographer when the time came . . ."

"Did you ever notice a copy of *The Euthanasia Handbook?*"

Martha was adamant. "Never! And I'd have said something if I had. It's God's will when we die."

Although she had several more questions, Carol filed them away for when she would have a better background and could therefore interrogate more effectively. She smiled agreeably as she said, "I'd appreciate a list of his friends and acquaintances, especially those he saw in the last month or so of his life."

Martha nodded soberly. "If one of them killed him," she said slowly, "I want them dead."

CHAPTER FOUR

They had hardly spoken the night before, so
when Carol came in from her usual morning run
through the quiet streets and the bushland skirting
the calm water of Middle Harbour, she was
determined to be affectionate and open.

Sybil, in jeans and a blue T-shirt, was leaning
against the kitchen bench sipping a cup of tea. Carol
sat down to unlace her running shoes. "Darling, I'm
sorry I was late last night..."

Putting her cup down carefully, Sybil said,
"There's something I want to talk to you about."

Her tone made Carol stop and look up. "Is it important?"

Sybil's face was remote, contained. "I think I mentioned the tenants in my house aren't renewing their lease. They left at the end of last week."

Carol thought she knew what was coming. She stared at ginger Jeffrey, Sybil's cat, who lay at her feet playing with one of her shoelaces. "You're thinking of moving back there?"

"Just for a while. Until we can sort things out."

Jeffrey was galvanized into evasive action as Carol abruptly stood up. Even Sinker, who had been sitting in a neat package under the chair, was prompted to move by Carol's raised voice. "You're going because of what I said over the invitation to Mark's wedding? I don't believe it!"

Sybil flushed with a corresponding anger. "Carol, of course it isn't just that. It's everything."

A feeling of baffled rage swept over Carol, but she kept her voice even. "Why do you always pick breakfast to bring these things up? Is it because you know I have to go to work?"

Sybil's reply was stinging. "It's because," she said, "it's the only bloody time you're not too tired or too preoccupied. And even then . . ." She broke off with a gesture of frustration. "This is pointless."

"Darling . . ."

"Let's talk about this later."

"You brought up the subject," Carol protested.

Sybil gave her a weary smile. "Yes, I did, didn't I? Stupid, really, since I always know what the outcome will be."

* * * * *

Ordinarily, Carol would have mentioned to Mark Bourke that she'd received his wedding invitation, but the subject was off-limits this morning. She frowned at him when he came jauntily into her office. "Yes?"

He raised his eyebrows at her tone. "Saw Raeburn's doctor this morning, but if you'd like to see me later . . ."

At his mild rebuke she felt an irritated guilt. "Now would be fine."

"First, I checked that the drugs Raeburn took in the hotel room were prescribed by his doctor—and they were, so there's nothing suspicious there." He referred to his notes. "Now, about the HIV. Raeburn wasn't a blood donor, so I presume he wouldn't have had any tests at all until the first signs of sickness turned up, except that his father was insisting that Collis take out a much heftier life insurance policy than the one he had."

"Beneficiaries if he died?"

"The family company would get the lot. Of course, once the HIV result came in, there was no way the insurance company was upping the payout to the requested million and a half, so Raeburn's life was insured for the original eight hundred thousand when he died. And you can see why his family want it to be an accidental death, because the existing policy has the usual clause voiding the contract in the case of suicide."

Carol played with her gold pen, a present from Sybil. "Raeburn didn't try to avoid the blood test?"

"Nope. The insurance company wanted a physical, including a blood test, before they'd increase the policy, so Raeburn went to his own doctor, apparently without the slightest idea there was any problem. His doctor says that he, himself, was astounded when the blood test indicated that Raeburn was HIV-positive. When he told him, Raeburn insisted on a second blood test. That showed the same result."

"Any idea how long he'd been carrying the virus?"

Bourke looked as though he'd eaten something bitter. "As far as I know, Raeburn wasn't showing any physical signs, but it varies so much from person to person. Could have been months, years even."

Carol began to doodle arrows on a scratch pad. "How'd he take it? Depression? Anger?"

"The doctor says he was reasonably calm. He listened to all the medical stuff, took the name of an AIDS counselor—who, incidentally, he never contacted—told his doctor he'd beat the virus and he was convinced a cure was around the corner, and went off into the sunset. His doctor never saw him again."

"He may have gone to an AIDS clinic where he'd have specialist medical help."

Bourke ran his hand over his hair. "Can you imagine," he said, "what it'd be like to walk in, thinking everything was okay, and be told you had a death sentence?"

Carol wondered what *she* would do. "It'd be rough, and all the worse when you had to tell friends or lovers that you might have infected them."

Sounding almost angry, Bourke said, "You say he told Martha Brownlye, but as far as I can see, that's it. Either he didn't warn anyone, or they're keeping quiet about it. The doctor told Raeburn he must warn any sexual partners, whether he practiced safe sex with them or not . . . it's not always that safe."

"There were no needle marks on the body, but he may have used intravenous drugs in the past."

Bourke's usually mild voice was harsh. "He was told to contact anyone he'd shared needles with, if he ever had."

Puzzled by the suppressed anger in Bourke's voice, Carol said, "Mark, there's something here I don't understand. Have you got a problem with this?"

"Sort of."

"What is it?"

"I don't want this to go any further." He looked up at her murmur of protest. "I'm sorry, Carol. It's just that it's a little close to home. Pat's younger brother, actually . . ." He rubbed his knuckles along his jaw. "The first he knew is when he got sick, really sick. He's progressed to early-stage AIDS and his immune system's stuffed. Tony had pneumonia a few weeks ago, although he seems okay at the moment."

"Oh, Mark . . ."

"He's really still just a kid—he's in his early twenties." He added bitterly, "It was an older man, married. He told Tony everything was okay, that he was clean, that it was quite safe. After all, the guy said to Tony, I'm not *gay,* just looking for something a little different . . ." He shook his head. "The bastard's probably infected his wife too."

"He might not have known."

Bourke's face was flushed with anger. "That's an excuse, is it? Tony's going to die, Carol, unless some miracle occurs. He won't ever see thirty. And it's all because someone just like Collis Raeburn was too selfish or too stupid to take precautions."

Carol wanted to cool his uncustomary anger. This new Mark Bourke had the uncomfortable shock of the unfamiliar. "Can we get back to Raeburn?"

"Sure." He gave her a fleeting smile. "Sorry—got a bit carried away there."

"Not at all, Mark. Did Raeburn discuss with his doctor how he caught the virus?"

"Not a word. He listened to the medical advice, refused to answer any personal questions, established the protocol about confidentiality, and left."

"We could try some of the AIDS clinics."

"We could, but they have an absolute ban on providing any information that could identify an HIV patient."

"See what you can dig up, Mark."

He unfolded himself from the chair. "Okay. But you know no one's going to want to talk. To lots of people HIV and AIDS are words that are the ultimate obscenities."

"What's more obscene," said Carol, "is that there may be people he slept with who are infected, and don't know it."

Carol noticed that Anne Newsome seemed to be treating her with unusual deference. As their car was waved through the gate at the Sydney Opera House, she glanced over at the young constable. Her short curly hair and olive skin shone with health and suppressed energy. Carol said mildly, "Perhaps

I'm wrong, but you seem to be treating me with rather elaborate courtesy."

Anne didn't bother to dissemble. Grinning, she said, "Thought you'd bite my head off if I didn't."

"That bad, eh?"

An anxiously obsequious official was waiting for them under the illuminated STAGE DOOR sign. This inappropriate appellation marked the cavernous entrance to the Opera House basement that was barred by a boom gate and flanked by a glass-walled room with uniformed security officers and an elaborate console of lights indicating the status of all areas of the building.

"Inspector Ashton! I'm Douglas Binns. We spoke on the phone? Afraid there's a minor problem. Lloyd Clancy and Alanna Brooks are still in rehearsal. I know you made firm appointments, and both of them should be free soon, but ... ah ..." He trailed off into a glum silence.

He was neat, nondescript and eager to please. When Carol said, "Is Corinne Jawalski available?" he brightened immediately.

"Indeed, yes. I left her in the Green Room, actually, a few minutes ago. She isn't due for rehearsal for some time, so if you'd follow me ..."

The Stage Door entry was the beginning of a huge square tunnel that bisected the building from south to north and was large enough to accommodate trucks and machinery. At the far end Carol could see the scintillating light reflected off the water of Sydney Harbour. Binns led them past forklifts, stage flats, anonymous piles of equipment, then plunged into a network of stairs and passages.

Over his shoulder he said, "I've been in touch with Edward Livingston's secretary since I last spoke with you, Inspector. I'm afraid Mr. Livingston can't make time to see you for a few days, at least."

He paused, seemingly embarrassed by his inability to deliver on schedule, but brightened as they entered a large rectangular room. Only a few people occupied an area that obviously could accommodate hundreds. At one end was a serving area with what looked like standard cafeteria food, at the other a wide window framed an arresting view of the harbor. Between these extremes of utility and beauty sat rows of tables and chairs like any communal eating space, and then, nearing the dazzling water, a lounge area and bar.

Smiling with obvious pride, he said, "The famous Green Room. You might be interested, Inspector, to know that seven hundred performers and staff eat here every day."

Carol repressed a smile. "Indeed?" she said.

He waved a proprietary hand. "And these monitors show each theater, so one can sit here and see one's cue on stage." He paused, apparently expecting some positive reaction from his audience.

Half-smiling, Carol looked at Anne Newsome, who obediently responded, "That's very interesting."

This seemed to be sufficient. He swept them towards a red lounge near the glare of the window where a slight figure in a plain white dress sat desultorily flipping the pages of a magazine. "Corinne?"

She looked up, sulky and unsmiling. "Yeah?"

"This is Detective Inspector Carol Ashton and

Constable Newsome." When she didn't respond, he went on, "Corinne Jawalski, one of our brightest young stars."

She came to her feet with one easy movement. Carol had the thought that she was one of those people who, although not beautiful, act as though they are. "You want to speak to me about Collis." Her voice had been assured until she said his name. She blinked quickly, obviously attempting to regain control.

A year before, Corinne Jawalski had had the good fortune to step into a major role at short notice when a flamboyant imported soprano had fallen suddenly ill. The fledgling diva was already known to the general public because she had won a television talent quest and had then gone on to be featured in a series of advertisements devoted to the Tourist Board's drive to depict Australia as a cultural identity rather than just a collection of scenic items. Unfazed by the searchlight of publicity, Corinne had sung Gilda in *Rigoletto* to spectacular effect, and her operatic career had moved into high gear.

At Carol's elbow, Binns was looking anxious. "Inspector, would you like me to find somewhere private . . ."

Carol glanced around the almost deserted Green Room. "It's only a few preliminary questions. Here will be fine, if it's all right with Ms Jawalski."

"Then I'll check on the rehearsal. I'm sure they'll be free soon. Be back shortly."

As he hurried away, Corinne gestured to an adjoining red couch. Any grief for Collis Raeburn she might have felt was hidden as she said crisply, "Might as well make yourself comfortable, Inspector. I've got a few things to say."

Dryly amused that her interrogation seemed to be in the process of being hijacked, Carol nodded to Anne to take her place, then obediently sat down. "Please go on."

Head tilted to one side, the young woman surveyed her. At last she said, "Is this really an investigation, or is it just going through the motions?"

"Meaning?"

Her voice had grown harsh. "Do I have to spell it out? Hush up the scandal and accentuate the tragedy. That sort of thing."

Carol gave her a brief ironic smile. "This is really an investigation. Now, what would you like to say?"

Corinne Jawalski pursed her lips. She had a plain, yet elegant face, heavy coils of rich brown hair and an aura of cool authority that was almost incongruous in one so young. "Next season, I was to be Collis's new partner. He was going to tell Edward Livingston that he didn't want Alanna singing with him anymore, at least in the roles that really need someone my age." She smoothed the skirt of her white dress. "Quite apart from the fact she was older than Collis, it looks ludicrous, don't you think, to have a middle-aged woman singing in *Romeo and Juliet*?"

Noting the thread of malice under the conversational tone, Carol wondered if she had been jealous of the other soprano. "They've been singing together for some time?"

"I suppose so."

Carol probed a little more. "They were friends?"

Corinne flushed slightly. "What has this got to do with anything?"

Carol said mildly, "I was wondering how he told her about this new arrangement."

She shrugged. "I've no idea if Alanna knew. Frankly, I don't know if he told anyone else, but that's what he was going to do. I mean, these things happen, don't they? Things change."

Carol said pleasantly, "Forgive me—I don't understand the ins and outs of your profession, but I would have thought decisions about casting would not be left to the singers . . ."

Corinne's tone was equally agreeable. "In most cases, of course not. But Collis could ask for anything . . . and he got it. It's one of the perks of fame, Inspector Ashton."

"Why was he thinking of replacing Alanna Brooks with you?"

The question elicited a complacent smile. "I don't like to sound immodest, but Collis believed we would make a better team. I mean, Alanna's had a great career, and she's not that old for a singer, but . . ."

"She's past it?" said Anne.

The young singer swung her attention to the constable. "Brutal," she said with a faint curve to her lips, "but pretty accurate. Alanna had it to begin with—there's no doubt of that—but her high notes are getting hard, the bloom's off her voice. She should have years of singing left, but . . ." She added with unconvincing regret, "Faulty technique, probably."

Such casual cruelty. Carol said, "When did you last speak with Collis Raeburn?"

73

The question jolted the young woman. Her expression of private triumph melted into misery. She dropped her head, saying almost inaudibly, "That evening."

"He called you from his hotel?"

"Collis didn't say where he was, but it must have been from the hotel. It was about seven and I was on my way out when my flatmate took the call. Beth called me back, but I was in a hurry, so we only had a short conversation."

"Why was he calling?"

"Why was he calling," Corinne repeated.

Repeating the question gives you time to think. What is it you need to think about? Carol looked over at Anne, and was pleased to see that she was watching Corinne Jawalski intently.

The young soprano put her hand to her mouth, then said with an attempt at nonchalance, "Nothing important. Just some stuff about Graeme Welton's latest little epic."

"*Dingo?* Were you to sing in it?"

"I wasn't tied to it legally, if that's what you mean. Poor Collis was packing death at the thought of the whole thing. Didn't want to be involved, and couldn't see how he could get out of it."

"Did Mr. Raeburn sound depressed?"

"Well, he wasn't very happy. I got the feeling Alanna was giving him a hard time."

"Because you were to replace her?"

The singer gave an offhand gesture. "Don't know. Could've been anything. Alanna's always taken the role of temperamental prima donna as far as she can to give her an excuse to bitch about anything and everything."

Carol looked up to see Binns approaching. She got to her feet. "Ms Jawalski, I'd appreciate it if you give Constable Newsome full details of the conversation—anything you can remember verbatim would be a help."

Binns was beaming. "Lloyd Clancy's in his dressing room right now. Can I take you down?"

Confident the young constable could complete the interview efficiently, Carol said to Corinne, "Please excuse me. Constable Newsome will have a few more questions for you and will make arrangements for a statement."

Plainly irked to find Carol leaving her midway through the interview, she said tartly, "There's a lot more you should know, Inspector."

"I'm sure we'll speak again."

Carol followed Binns as he plunged into a low-roofed wide corridor. Brightly lit, filled with the muffled hum of air-conditioning and carpeted with gray-brown carpet chosen to blend in with the widest range of stains, it seemed identical to all other corridors she had seen in the Opera House. "Do you ever get lost?"

He was delighted with her question. "No, but I can see how you might think that. It's the white birch ply." At her raised eyebrows, he elaborated, "This blond wood you see everywhere. It's in all the passageways, the rooms. Native wood of New South Wales, white birch. Makes everything look the same."

As they came to a halt outside a pale door labeled *Mr. Clancy*, Binns pointed to a row of huge wicker containers that filled half the corridor. "They're called skips. It's traditional to transport all the costumes and props in them."

The door opened to his diffident knock. Carol had seen Lloyd Clancy in photographs and on television, but she wasn't prepared for the full weight of his engaging personality. Rather heavily built and with an imposingly hooked nose, deeply set dark eyes and a rougish smile, he radiated a cheeky informality. He was wearing ancient jeans and a navy blue shirt. "Come in, Inspector Ashton," he said with an elaborate sweeping gesture. "I find it very reassuring that you're on the case."

"Indeed?"

"Absolutely indeed!" He was chuckling at her skeptical tone as he ushered her down a tiny hallway with a cramped bathroom on one side and a walk-in wardrobe on the other. The dressing room itself was quite small, one side of it taken up with makeup mirrors ringed with lights. Set into another wall was a control panel from which music and singing whispered. "The rehearsal," he said, as she glanced at it. "I'm due back for the next act, so I'll know when I have to be there." Seating her on a rather battered lounge, he said to Binns, "Douglas, coffee would be wonderful. Could you?"

The dressing room had the ubiquitous gray-brown carpet and pale cream woodwork and walls. The window was a long oblong laid on its side through which an expanse of water danced in the sunlight. Seeing her watching a catamaran ferry swishing past, he said, "Lovely view, isn't it? Unfortunately, I hardly have time to appreciate it, and besides, one can become accustomed to too much beauty, don't you agree?"

"Perhaps, although the harbor's changing all the time."

The amusement disappeared from his face. His voice was washed of laughter as he said, "Yes, everything changes. You want to see me about Collis." He'd taken one of the three-wheeled swivel-backed chairs from the makeup mirror, swung it around so the back faced him, and had straddled it. Now he sat, hands folded along the top of the backrest, watching her closely.

"Let's start with how he was the last time you saw or spoke with him."

Clancy's initial levity had vanished. He said pensively, "I can't believe we're sitting here discussing Collis's death. It's such a pity . . ."

"When did you see him?" Carol prompted.

"Would have been about midafternoon on that final day. He was here, in this dressing room. Wanted to check something about next month's schedule. Seemed preoccupied, but not depressed. Of course, you couldn't always tell with Collis. He was an intensely private man."

"Did you get on well?"

This question earned a rueful smile. "To be honest, not particularly." He seemed to make an effort to be jocular. "I mean, it's no secret we were rivals. Tenors often are." He added disarmingly, "In opera we have all these noble, heroic parts, you see. And all this drama spills over into our lives."

What are you really feeling? Are you happy that your challenger has gone? She said lightly, "So the stereotyped perception of the opera world is correct? It *is* seething with professional jealousy?"

He tried to match her tone. "Positively boiling."

"And Collis Raeburn? Where was he in all of this?"

Clancy's smile disappeared. "He was heading for the very top. Superstardom, internationally. It wasn't just the voice, plenty of singers have that. What made Collis different was his drive, his determination, his eye for the main chance. Oh, and a theatrical sense. His PR person didn't hinder him, either."

"Who is that?"

"Anita Burgess. You'd have heard of her."

Carol had. Ex-wife of a prominent politician, she had used every contact he had made in public life to establish her public relations consultancy as one of the most successful small agencies in Australia.

Clancy went on, "And success like Collis's made a lot of people very envious. Some wanted to pull him down, some wanted to hitch a ride on his coattails . . ."

"What did you want to do?" asked Carol blandly.

He gave her a mocking look. "Why, Inspector, surely you realize I'm a success in my own right?" He added, "You might like to think of us as twin rockets, our careers ascending to the skies."

"Is that how you saw it?"

"I envied Raeburn's success," he said soberly. "It was unfortunate that my career coincided with his, because it seemed inevitable that he would overshadow me. But that's all it was—envy. I didn't wish him harm, and on a professional level we got along perfectly well. I can say quite sincerely that I regret his death deeply, because he had a magnificent voice, and he'd hardly begun, in operatic terms, to realize his potential."

"You mention a professional level. How about a personal level?"

A cynical smile. "Hated his guts," said Lloyd Clancy.

Douglas Binns was apologetic. "Alanna Brooks has come down with a severe migraine headache. She's in her dressing room, but I don't know if she can give you an interview."

The prima donna's dressing room was the twin of Lloyd Clancy's, but the curtains had been drawn to shut out the light and the beauty of the harbor. Alanna Brooks's full-figured body was huddled in a chair, her head resting on one hand. The fair, translucent skin of her face was drawn. She said, her voice husky, "Inspector Ashton, I'm sorry, but I've asked Douglas to call a cab. When I get one of these migraines, it's the full disaster—pain, vision disturbances and nausea. The only thing that helps is to lie down and go to sleep. I realize you need to speak with me, but I'm afraid it's impossible at the moment."

"Would you just tell me when you last saw or spoke to Mr. Raeburn?"

Alanna Brooks groped around in a bag and found a pair of sunglasses. As she put them on, she said, "God. I feel terrible."

"Ms Brooks?"

"Yes, Collis . . . I saw him on Saturday afternoon, here in the dressing room. He didn't say or do anything to make me think he was going to do what he did."

Douglas Binns knocked. "The cab's here."

The diva stood carefully. "I think my head's going

to explode . . . Inspector, can I call you tomorrow? I'll see you as soon as I can."

"Handy headache?" said Carol to Anne Newsome as they walked to the car.

"Perhaps she needs time to counter the less than flattering comments Corinne Jawalski continued to make after you'd left us," said Anne. "She was reasonably civil about male singers, but mention a rival soprano and she's in for the kill."

"It's becoming obvious to me that opera's just like the Police Service," observed Carol. "You have to watch your back, because your colleagues can be dangerous."

She ignored Anne's surprised expression, wondering herself why she'd expressed this thought in words.

Changing to a strictly-business tone, she said, "Did you ask Corinne about her personal relationship with Raeburn?"

"Her actual words," said Anne with a smile, "were that they were close friends and colleagues."

"Believe her?"

Anne shook her head. "Underneath all that venom," she said, "I think there's a real grief. It's possible she loved him."

"Yes, and let's follow that up. I've got something else for you to do. *The Euthanasia Handbook* is shrink-wrapped in plastic and anyone buying a copy has to be over eighteen. Most bookshops ask for a current driver's license." She caught Anne's unenthusiastic expression, and smiled. "Yes, I know it's a long shot, but I would like a check made of bookshops where Raeburn might conceivably have bought a copy in, say, the last couple of months. He's very well known, particularly from television, so it's possible someone will remember him. And if we can find that he definitely did buy the handbook, that will strengthen the possibility of suicide."

"His fingerprints were on the book."

Carol caught at a thought she hadn't put into action. "Yes, Anne, the fingerprints. The book was marketed sealed in plastic, so it could be expected that his would be the only prints on it. I'm interested in exactly where he touched the handbook—it seems such a convenient prop for a suicide scene." She smiled as she added, "And in case you have time to spare, I'd like you to see Raeburn's publicist, Anita Burgess. Also, see if you can speak to Corinne Jawalski's flatmate. I'd be interested to know if she did have a call from Raeburn, and when."

"Want to speak with Pat?" said Bourke as she walked in. "I'm taking her to lunch, and I asked her to be early in case you were in the market for first-hand opera gossip."

Because of the engagement, Carol had become friendly with Pat and found herself growing genuinely fond of her, not only because of her frank, open nature, but also because she had so obviously made Mark Bourke happy. "When will Pat be here?"

"Half an hour or so."

"Great. I'll take her out for coffee and you can

pick her up from there." She added mischievously, "I suppose this a wedding-talk lunch?"

"Don't think I can cope," he said, laughing. "I just can't believe how many arrangements have to be made just to get hitched."

Carol was about to make a snide comment about first-time grooms but caught herself. Bourke had been married before, had lost his wife and child in a boating accident. It was something he'd never spoken about to her, but she knew the tragedy must have cast a permanent shadow over his life. She imagined what it would be like if her own son were to die. She loved David unconditionally. He was the only individual she had ever permitted herself to love so totally, and she was still bitterly regretful that she had ever allowed herself to be persuaded to give him up.

"Getting married's easy," she said mockingly. "It's what happens afterwards that's hard to cope with."

"Thanks for the confidence boost." He handed her a telephone message. "Madeline Shipley called. She wants you to ring her back as soon as possible."

Carol was surprised by the twinge of excitement she felt at Madeline's name. "Did she say why?"

He snorted. "We both know why. She's part of the feeding frenzy over Collis Raeburn, and she's going to use the fact she knows you personally the best way she knows how."

One of Australia's most successful television personalities, Madeline Shipley hosted the consistently high-rated *Shipley Report,* strip-scheduled early evening where the competition was ferocious, in an attempt to snare viewers for the rest of the night. Television's demands, as far as female presenters were concerned, made it mandatory that Madeline Shipley be physically attractive and personally charming, but she was much more than this: intelligent, inquisitive, and when necessary, ruthless. Her slight build held a willpower like tungsten and a tenacity that had defeated the most difficult interviewees.

And, for Carol, Madeline held one other potent attraction—she was one of the few people Carol could relax with concerning her private life. She not only knew about Carol and Sybil, she also understood—being so firmly in the closet herself—the tightrope act of balancing professional and private lives. She shared with Carol the same conviction: "Announce publicly that you're a lesbian, and to your face people will say how brave you are to stop living a lie and how much they admire you. Then you wave goodbye to your career."

As she dialed Madeline Shipley's private line, Carol realized that she was actively looking forward to hearing Madeline's voice, her lazy, beguiling laugh.

Madeline answered at the third ring. "Carol? Why haven't I seen you lately? How's Sybil?"

It was a loaded question, though Madeline couldn't know this. "Sybil's fine."

A slight pause, then Madeline said with an indefinable note in her voice, "That's good."

Carol could visualize Madeline's quizzical expression. Wanting to short-circuit any further personal questions, she said, "What can I do for you?"

Madeline chuckled at Carol's businesslike tone. "No time for idle chitchat, eh? Well, Carol, you know very well what you can do for me. You may know we've been preparing a TV special about Collis Raeburn and the Eureka Opera Company. Deadlines have become rather more urgent with his death, so I'm asking for absolutely every gruesome detail you can give me."

"This is where you get the standard reply."

"No it isn't," said Madeline with conviction. "I've got something to trade. Have dinner with me tonight after the show and I'll tell you some very interesting things."

Carol found herself smiling. *I really want to see her.* "How do I know it'll be worth my while?"

"One little phrase should do it," said Madeline. "How about 'HIV-positive'?"

CHAPTER FIVE

Edward Livingston's personal assistant seemed accustomed to parrying irksome requests. "I'm sorry, Inspector, but Mr. Livingston cannot come to the phone at the moment, and I'm not sure when he'll be available. I'd be pleased to pass on a message."

Carol said formally, "I'm investigating the circumstances of Collis Raeburn's death. Information given to me in confidence regarding Mr. Livingston leads me to believe he can materially assist this investigation. For that reason I need to see him as soon as possible."

"I'm sorry, but—" The voice broke off, to be replaced by a rich baritone.

"Inspector Ashton? Someone's been gossiping about me, have they?"

So he'd been unable to resist the bait. Carol made arrangements to meet the controversial opera manager mid-afternoon.

"Look, Inspector, let's make it neutral territory. How about the cafe on the broadwalk in front of the Opera House? We can sit out in the sun and share our secrets with the seagulls."

She was leaning back in her chair considering the questions she intended to ask when Mark Bourke brought Pat James into her office, an embarrassed pride in his manner. Carol was warmed to see the affection on his face as he smiled at his future wife.

In a little over a week, Carol would be watching these two exchange their vows for a life together. What irony—the ceremony that would link Pat and Mark was the point of conflict that had driven Sybil to leave. Carol couldn't separate the ache of loss from the confused anger she felt.

"Ready?" Pat said to Carol.

Pat James emanated the buoyant good health that Carol always, for some reason, associated with involvement with team games such as basketball or hockey, and, in general, to being a "good sport." She was tall, close to the same height as Bourke, but whereas his solid build made him a definite, heavy physical presence, Pat's light frame seemed springy and resilient.

She grinned at Carol. "Let's blow the joint and do coffee, eh? Oxford Street?"

Collecting her things, Carol said, "Mark, we'll be at the usual place. Pick Pat up when you're ready for lunch."

"I'm ready now."

"You're not, you know. I want more details on Edward Livingston and his financial situation . . . and I'd like you to come with me this afternoon, since I've pinned him down for an interview."

Oxford Street was its usual busy mix of nationalities, sexual orientations and colorfully eccentric personalities. This first section of the busy street had a certain seedy enthusiasm, a bohemian acceptance of differences; however, after it flowed past the sandstone law courts in Taylor Square, the money of fashionable Paddington began to dilute and refine its raw vitality.

The coffee shop was Italian—clean, cramped and dominated by a fiendishly hissing coffee machine. After ordering black coffee for herself and cappuccino for Pat, Carol said, "What are people saying about Collis Raeburn's death?"

"The arts world's abuzz. Last night we had a cocktail party at the Gallery to launch a new exhibition of Asian artifacts, and believe me, Collis Raeburn was the main topic of conversation. Mind, no one has any hard information, but that little detail has never stopped gossip before."

Wincing as Pat stirred three heaped teaspoons of sugar into her coffee, Carol decided that the word that best described Pat James was good-humored.

She smiled readily, and, when really amused, guffawed. She had an irreverent, frank approach that seemed at odds with the artistic and cultural world in which she moved because of her position at the Art Gallery of New South Wales.

Pat took a sip of her coffee, made a face, then stirred it vigorously. "There's very real grief at his death. He really had the most extraordinary voice..." A thought suddenly amused her. "Carol, like a bet? Ten dollars says someone at Raeburn's funeral says, 'We shall not see his like again.' You on?"

"I never bet against sure things."

Pat looked at her thoughtfully. "No doubt the Raeburn family are pulling strings. Kenneth Raeburn is a ruthless little bastard who likes to throw his weight around, although I have heard that his son was about to dump him."

Astonished, Carol said, "Dump him how?"

"From the family company. Collis Raeburn employed his father and sister to run his career and handle the financial side of things, but Kenneth has a lot more arrogance than good sense, and Collis was talking of bringing in a professional manager. This could've been embarrassing for his father, since there'd be an audit. My guess is that Kenneth Raeburn's business skills would have been found seriously wanting."

"So Collis's death would get him off the hook?"

Pat grinned sardonically. "Although Mark won't tell me anything about the investigation, the word around the traps is that you've been put on the case because you have high credibility and if you say it was all a nasty accident, who will contradict you?"

Carol wanted to say, *Do you really believe I'm for hire? That I'd compromise myself that way?* But to put it into words would be to imply she believed Pat might think it possible . . .

"It's manifestly clear," said Pat scornfully, "that a nice, clean accidental death would be the best result for the family, especially one that only involves prescription drugs."

"Meaning?"

"Collis was supposed to be a very good client for drugs, principally cocaine. It seems a popular theory that he accidentally killed himself with a cocktail of illegal substances. Then there's the clique that just knows he died from unrequited love."

"For whom?"

"Carol, I do admire your grammar!" She took a sip of coffee, then grew more serious. "Supposedly, he'd been having an affair with Corinne Jawalski, but some people think it was a smokescreen for his *real* affair with Graeme Welton. And, to add a little spice to the pot, it's rumored that early in his career he had quite a steamy romance with Alanna Brooks."

Signaling for two more coffees, Carol said, "Surely a tenor having a romance with his prima donna is standard public relations stuff. Doesn't have to be true, but it adds piquancy to the duets."

"Who would have thought you such a cynic!"

"Who indeed," Carol said with a grin. "Was there any comment about Edward Livingston? He's doing his best to avoid seeing me."

"Edward Livingston—impresario extraordinaire! If he were only half as good as he thinks he is, the Eureka Opera Company would be as highly regarded as the Australian Opera." She grinned at Carol's questioning expression. "No, I haven't got a personal grudge, it's just that he takes himself so *seriously,* and when something goes wrong with one of his magnificent schemes to revitalize opera, it's never *his* fault—it's always somebody else who's spoilt it for him. For instance, he was bitterly angry when his loony television version of *Madame Butterfly* slumped in the ratings after he'd promoted it like a football match. Naturally, he had to blame someone, so he turned on Collis and accused him of sabotaging the whole thing by singing the role of Pinkerton, extraterrestrial, so badly."

Thinking how much she'd hate to work in an atmosphere of such high drama, Carol said, "I've been given the impression that the clash of personalities is fairly common in the opera world."

Pat chortled. "Egos are not in short supply. Even so, successful artists, whatever field they're in, have to be professional, or they don't last long. Means there's often thunder and lightning, but not much rain. It's always been different, though, with our Edward. He's one of the great grudge-bearers of the twentieth century, and Collis had crossed him once too often."

"They were in open conflict?"

"Very. There've been veiled references to the stoush in all the newspaper arts' columns for weeks now. Livingston's penchant for suing for defamation made sure that no one actually named him, but everyone knew they'd fallen out and Collis was going to do his best to get out of his contract with Eureka."

Carol took a reflective sip of coffee. "I've also heard about conflict with a rival. What about Lloyd Clancy?"

"Ah," said Pat enthusiastically, "what about Lloyd Clancy, indeed? One society matron, whose name would surprise you, confided to me that in her circle it's understood that Lloyd assisted Collis to join the heavenly choir in the sky."

"Murdered him, or helped him suicide?"

"Either. And before you ask for a motive, bear in mind that opera is a high pressure, demanding world, where you make sweet music on stage, and play management politics off it. Only winners really prosper. The also-rans end up in the chorus, are doomed to subsidiary roles, or skitter off to less demanding singing careers. Lloyd's older than Collis, and he'd established his career, but he was slowly but surely being overhauled."

Carol played with a sachet of artificial sweetener. "Are you seriously suggesting that's an adequate motive for a murder?"

Pat laughed. "Carol, you know I'm never serious, but if I were, I'd point you in the direction of Nicole Raeburn. If ever anyone burned with incestuous love, she did."

"If that's so, was it returned?" asked Carol, remembering the sister's disturbing intensity.

"Who knows? But whether it was or not, that woman's unbalanced. It's hardly an exaggeration to say that Collis was a god to her."

"Then she wouldn't want him dead," said Carol mildly.

"If she happened to be jealous enough, she might," said Pat with conviction. "And there's none so ferocious as an acolyte scorned."

Feeling positively awash with coffee, Carol refused more when Edward Livingston joined her at the round white table shaded by a central umbrella. The early days of spring hinted at the lazy summer days to come, the sun having a warm weight that tempered the chill of the breeze off the water. Seagulls were preoccupied with noisy courtships, or with harassing anyone who had food. The other tables were occupied by assorted tourists who basked in the sun, took photographs or rested weary feet. Behind the broadwalk the spectacular curved roofs of the Opera House soared, pale against an azure sky. In front of them the harbor danced with light and activity and to their left the gray skeleton of the Harbour Bridge spanned the gulf from south to north like a gigantic metal coat hanger.

"Nice weather," said Livingston.

"Almost like summer," replied Carol accommodatingly.

He chuckled at her tone. "Enough of the pleasantries. Let's get down to business. Just what stories have you heard concerning me?"

Controversial he might be, Carol thought, but he looked very like the stereotype of an accountant. He wore a conservative charcoal-gray suit with a deep green silk tie, his brown hair was cut neatly short, and, apart from a thin white scar that zigzagged down one cheek, his face was unremarkable. His most notable feature was his voice, a deep resonant baritone that he swelled and faded like an instrument, although even short acquaintance with his vocal technique had begun to irritate Carol.

She said, "When was your last contact with Collis Raeburn?"

"Oh, I don't know . . . a week before he died, probably."

Carol raised her eyebrows. "It surprises me you can't be a little more exact. Sudden death generally sharpens memories of final meetings."

"Of course I bow to your superior knowledge in these matters, Inspector, but frankly I'm very busy, I really can't recall. My assistant may have the information in my appointment book . . ."

"If his death shouldn't turn out to be suicide, would that surprise you?"

"Is there any doubt Collis killed himself?"

Countering with another question, Carol said, "Do *you* have any doubt?"

Livingston had kept very still up till this point, but now he began to run his fingers up and down the scar on his cheek. "Collis was an artist. Being unstable comes with the territory."

"Do you really believe that?"

Seeming to force himself to appear relaxed, he leaned back in his chair as he made an open-handed gesture. "Inspector, I deal with these people every day of the week. To their adoring public they're larger-than-life personalities with the world at their feet, but to me they're children, demanding attention, showing off, wanting the limelight."

Privately wondering how many cliches Edward Livingston could pack into one sentence, Carol said,

"Collis Raeburn certainly wasn't lacking attention and limelight."

"Yes, but that's what drove him to success," said Livingston almost smugly. "Collis was never, *ever* satisfied. He couldn't have too much recognition—fame was like a drug to him. The more he got, the more he wanted."

She didn't let her impatience show, although she was convinced she was hearing a well-worn routine that Livingston had used many times before. "So why would he kill himself?" she said baldly.

Livingston pursed his lips judiciously. "Collis's professional life was outstandingly successful. His personal life, however, was not."

Carol waited.

"Inspector Ashton, you must appreciate that grand opera creates a hothouse atmosphere. Emotions, hatreds, passions—all exaggerated, larger than life. Alanna Brooks has partnered Collis for many years, and they were good friends. But then, a younger, and very talented, soprano appears on the scene . . ."

"Corinne Jawalski," said Carol, obligingly filling in his pause.

"Corinne quite cold-bloodedly set out to have an affair with Collis, so that she could talk him into replacing Alanna with herself as his diva. Unfortunately, Collis fell for Corinne in a big way. Frankly, I tried to warn him, but he brushed me aside. I said she was just using him as a convenient way to leapfrog any rivals, but he was so besotted with her he was furious with me for criticizing her."

"Would she be able to supplant Alanna Brooks so easily?"

He gave a sharp laugh. "Oh, Corinne was sure of it, but it was unlikely, as I had the final say."

"I got the impression that someone of Raeburn's stature would have some clout . . ." She waited to see how he would respond.

His mouth tightened. "Wishful thinking, in most cases. I'm always willing to accommodate reasonable requests, but Alanna is a guaranteed draw-card—Corinne's still on the way up, and she may never make it to the top. More than that, there's a difference in voice quality. Corinne has a brilliant, light soprano, with a wide range and a beautiful top register—but it's a young voice. Alanna's voice is mature, although her range may have contracted slightly. But offsetting this is the rich palette of tonal qualities she has available."

"Does this mean you would favor Alanna Brooks?"

The question seemed to irritate him. "Probably," he snapped.

Carol said mildly, "So the choice of diva was a point of conflict between you and Mr. Raeburn?"

"That's too strong," he said emphatically. "I told you, Collis didn't like the criticism, that's all."

As he was speaking, Carol saw Mark Bourke approaching. She introduced him to Livingston, who smiled briefly, then ostentatiously checked his watch. "Inspector, Sergeant—I really don't have much time . . ."

Bourke unzipped a thin brown briefcase. "Mr. Livingston," he said pleasantly, "I wonder if you'd care to comment on some financial matters."

Livingston looked astonished. "Financial matters?"

"Also some legal undertakings," said Bourke. "We understand you'd had preliminary talks with your lawyers about a possible attempt by Raeburn to break his contract with Eureka Opera, and, more specifically, the legal obligation he had to sing the lead in Welton's *Dingo*."

"These were mere administrative matters." Livingston's full baritone swelled with indignation.

"He was Eureka's major star, wasn't he?" When Livingston reluctantly nodded, Bourke went on, "I imagine if he left the company, you would find it a financial, as well as a professional, loss?"

"I imagine so."

Carol said, "We've been told he was very unhappy about Graeme Welton's new opera."

"Collis was a singer," Livingston snapped, "not a composer. He was in no position to judge the success or otherwise of *Dingo*."

"Kenneth Raeburn told me the opera was, to quote him, an unmitigated disaster," said Carol, curious to see what impact the mention of Collis's father might have.

"Kenneth Raeburn," Livingston sneered, "is a jumped-up little prick who had the good fortune to have a son who could sing. And he's milked it for all it's worth. Why don't you have a look at *his* financial dealings? Think you'll find he's been taking Collis for a ride for years."

Bourke consulted some papers. "Would it be true to say that Eureka is close to bankruptcy?"

"No, it would not! Grand opera's a massively expensive business, Sergeant, that's why companies need government and sponsorship support. Eureka's no different from any other artistic or cultural body in Australia in that respect."

"But wouldn't a battle in the courts with one of your major stars not only be expensive in terms of legal costs, but also affect future corporate support for the company?"

Glaring at Bourke, Livingston said, "There wasn't going to be a battle! I spoke to Collis and we settled our differences. He was quite happy to sing the lead in *Dingo*."

Carol made sure she sounded politely skeptical. "So all your problems with Collis were resolved?"

"Yes."

"He doesn't seem to have told anyone else about your agreement on these matters."

Livingston made an impatient gesture. "He would hardly have had time, Inspector. We spoke on the day he died."

"This astonishes me a little," said Carol, "since only a few minutes ago you couldn't remember the last time you spoke to him. You thought it was a week or so ago . . ."

Livingston straightened his silk tie. "Frankly, Inspector, " he said with a tight smile, "I'd hoped to avoid any discussion of this fight with Collis. I mean, it didn't reflect well on him, and after the tragedy I thought it wrong to bring up something that had, with his death, become quite academic."

"So it was a deliberate lie?"

"Well, if you want to put it in those terms, yes. But not one that did any harm, you understand."

"On the contrary, Mr. Livingston. If, as you say, this major area of conflict *had* been resolved, then that would have some bearing on his state of mind."

"Inspector Ashton, you must forgive me," he said,

his change of tone indicating he was hastily making amends. "I'm very sorry if I've misled you in any way."

"When and where did you speak to Raeburn?"

Her cool tone seemed to subdue him. "During the afternoon. I'm not sure of the exact time, but it was here, in the Opera House, before he checked into his hotel."

"Before or after he spoke with Lloyd Clancy?"

Livingston fingered his scar. "I can't tell you that."

Carol thought Mark Bourke looked relaxed, disarming as he said, "And I suppose no one else was present?"

"No. No one."

"And you didn't tell anyone about this?"

"I would have done so, but when he died..."

"Ah yes, when he died," said Bourke with polite regret. "Now let's get this straight. You spoke to Raeburn on Saturday afternoon, and the earliest you could have known about his death was Monday. I don't understand why you didn't give the good news about *Dingo* to Graeme Welton."

"I didn't get around to it...And it was the weekend, too..."

"Would you say that you and Graeme Welton were good friends?"

Livingston stared at Carol. "Friends? More colleagues, I'd say. Why?" Before she could respond, he added furiously, "What's he been saying about me? He's a congenital liar, you know. Whatever story he's fed you, it isn't true."

Ignoring his outburst, Bourke said, "Would you

mind outlining your movements for Saturday and Sunday?"

"Why?"

Bourke sounded faintly surprised. "To assist our inquiries, of course."

Nicole Raeburn, accompanied by a frowning, fidgeting Graeme Welton, and with Anne Newsome standing guard, sat waiting when Carol got back. Carol showed them into her office, then had a private word with Anne.

"Did you find the journal Martha Brownlye mentioned?"

"No. It isn't with the papers taken from the house. I called Martha and asked her to check with Kenneth Raeburn, in case he took it, but he says he didn't touch it. I got a full description in case we'd overlooked it in all the stuff brought in, but I've double-checked and it's definitely disappeared."

The anonymous public-service furniture and serviceable colors of Carol's office provided a bland background to Nicole Raeburn's bright candy-pink dress and her highly dramatic gestures. "Inspector Ashton! I just had to see you!" She added with a petulant frown, her heavy head of hair tilted on a too-thin neck, "They wouldn't let us in, downstairs. Said it was security, or something, but I made a fuss and your constable came and got Welty and me. I like her. What's her name?"

"Detective Constable Anne Newsome."

Nicole giggled. "Did you use the title to remind

us that you're police officers?" she said archly. She turned to Welton. "Do you feel a little bit intimidated, Welty?"

Graeme Welton looked as though he was there on sufferance. He made an indeterminate sound and sat back in his chair, his fingers tapping a double tattoo on the armrests.

Nicole Raeburn was wearing what Carol categorized as a "little girl" dress, with many fussy adornments of ruffles and ribbons. Together with her extreme thinness, her attire made her seem very young and defenseless, although by Carol's calculations she would be at least thirty.

"How can I help you?" said Carol, sitting down behind the familiar protection of her desk, conscious that she felt an instinctive aversion to Raeburn's sister.

"We want to know what's going on about Colly."

Carol's dislike made her cordial. She said gently, "My report will be seen by the Commissioner, and it will then go to the Coroner to assist him with the inquest into your brother's death. None of it will be made public until that point."

"I'm his sister! I have a right to know everything!"

"I'm sorry. I'll have to refer you to my Chief Inspector, or to the Commissioner."

"I'll tell Auntie Marge!"

Carol couldn't imagine the new Minister for Police would welcome being dragged in to mediate. She let the childish threat hang in the air while she assessed Nicole's state of mind. Her agitated movements and wide-eyed stare suggested hysteria, but Carol was convinced that this display was an attempt to manipulate the situation to her own advantage.

Welton was squirming in his chair. "Nicole, just get to the point." Again, Carol was struck by the incongruity of such a high, light voice coming from such a powerful body.

His impatience had an effect on Nicole. She glared at him, then turned to Carol. "Inspector, I'd appreciate some kind of progress report about my brother."

Carol said mildly, "Under the circumstances, I'd be prepared to answer your questions, if I can."

She was wryly amused when Nicole appeared gratified by this seeming concession, as she had no intention of revealing anything other than the most general of observations.

"So when are you going to prove it was an awful accident? Daddy's so upset about the publicity, and it'll die down once you come up with the truth."

"We haven't completed our inquiries. In any case the inquest will determine what happened." Obviously this answer didn't satisfy Nicole, but before she could comment, Carol went on, "I'd like to ask if you ever saw your brother with a copy of *The Euthanasia Handbook.*"

"No."

As Nicole sat tight-lipped after this bald reply, Carol tried another tack. "During my inquiries I've heard a rumor that your brother took cocaine . . ."

Welton's tapping fingers stilled; Nicole gave a theatrical shrug as she said, "So?"

"He did use cocaine?"

It was clear Nicole considered the subject of little importance. "In the circles Colly moved, it was just

101

taken for granted." She added with a superior smile, "Like *you'd* use alcohol, with your friends."

"Mr. Welton?"

He smoothed his hair. "I don't know anything about it."

"Welty, that isn't true!"

He turned to Carol for understanding. "Inspector Ashton, you know there are always drugs around. Anything used was purely recreational. No one's into it in any serious way, and Collis certainly wasn't. He valued his voice too much to do anything to jeopardize it."

"Do either of you know who supplied him?"

Her face twisted. "*I* don't! And what's this got to do with him dying? Isn't that the important thing?" Her eyes filled with tears; there was a rising note of hysteria in her voice. "I miss him so! You don't know how I feel!"

She seemed to calm down when Graeme Welton leaned over to pat her hand. "Come on, Nikky, don't upset yourself."

Sympathy struggled with exasperation in Carol. "I'm sorry, Ms Raeburn. This must be very painful for you."

Rubbing her eyes with her knuckles, Nicole said, "Have you seen Lloyd Clancy? Everyone knows he hated Colly."

"Yes, I've interviewed Mr. Clancy."

"Well? Where was he when Colly died? Do you know?"

Repressing a sigh, Carol said, "Because your brother's body wasn't discovered until some considerable time had elapsed, the time of his death is impossible to pinpoint accurately."

"So alibis don't matter?"

The shrewdness under her childish persona still surprised Carol. "We're trying to narrow the possible time frame. For example, your telephone conversation with him in the early evening establishes that he was still conscious at that time."

"Does it matter, since it was a dreadful accident?" she demanded peevishly.

Carol's reply was matter-of-fact. "If it was an accident—probably not. If murder—yes."

"*Murder?* It was an accident! It couldn't have been anything else. When are you going to see that?" When Carol didn't respond, she demanded, "Why won't you give me straight answers? I'm entitled to know!"

"There's very little I *can* tell you, Ms Raeburn, at this point."

Nicole stood, righteously angry. "Come on, Welty. This is a waste of time."

"Mr. Welton, I'd like to speak with you for a moment," said Carol, smoothly interposing.

Nicole pouted. "You can ask anything in front of me. We're friends, after all."

Carol gestured to Anne Newsome. "Constable, would you see Ms Raeburn out, please."

Left alone with Carol, Graeme Welton looked embarrassed. "Look, Inspector, I'm sorry about the way Nikky behaved. She's really stressed by what's happened . . ."

"I understand that. Please sit down." After he'd complied, Carol said, "Mr. Welton, during an investigation there are times when we have to ask very personal questions . . ."

Looking resigned, he said, "Go on, then. Ask."

"I'd like some more details about your association with Collis Raeburn. Specifically, did you have a sexual relationship with him?"

His hands, that had been weaving an elaborate dance with each other, stilled. "Yes, I'm afraid so," he said.

"Afraid?"

Welton passed a hand over his face. "Collis was the most selfish person I've ever met. He put himself first, second, third and last—and all the places in between. Any relationships to him were there to bolster his ego." He looked up at her, his piercingly blue eyes dimmed by unshed tears. "But when I heard he was dead, I didn't think I could bear it."

"Were you surprised he'd killed himself?"

The question elicited a mirthless smile. "Very. Collis was convinced that he was the most glorious thing he had ever known, so why would he destroy himself?"

CHAPTER SIX

Carol sat in her office mentally reviewing the case as she absentmindedly played with her gold pen. She looked at its embossed metal shaft, thinking that it had been a birthday present from Sybil. She put it down gently. *I'm not going to think about that now.*

Mark was always on time, but Anne hurried in a little late. Once they were seated, she said, "Okay troops. Report time."

"You're in a good mood," Mark said.

Carol gave him a brief smile. "We're getting there, Mark. I'm beginning to see a pattern."

"So it's murder."

"It's murder," she said with confidence. "All right, Anne, what've you got?"

As Anne Newsome opened a folder and cleared her throat, Carol remembered the feeling of importance she herself had felt the first time she'd been entrusted with a strand of an investigation. Anne's reporting technique was admirably succinct as she briefly described her interview with Anita Burgess, Raeburn's publicist. "They had a professional relationship, but she says she knows nothing about his personal life ... If she actually does, she isn't saying."

"You interviewed Corinne Jawalski's flatmate?"

"Yes, Beth Adkins. It's just as we were told—Mr. Raeburn called about seven, asked for Corinne, who had just walked out the door. Beth called her back and she talked to him for a few minutes." Anne's manner made it clear she had something of significance to add. "One thing Jawalski *didn't* tell us is that it was more an argument than a conversation. Beth says she doesn't know what it was about, but it ended with Corinne slamming the receiver down, letting go with a few choice words about Raeburn, then stalking off."

Carol leaned forward. "And her movements after that?"

"Just as she said: she went with a friend to the Town Hall for a performance of *Elijah*. He was a soloist in the oratorio, so he was up on the stage while Corinne was in the audience. The performance started at eight and he didn't see her again until after ten-thirty."

Carol smiled at Anne's anticipatory expression. "So what do you get from that?"

"Why, that she had time to go to the hotel and see Collis Raeburn. She wasn't sitting in the audience with anyone who knew her, and she could catch a bus, or taxi, or even walk—it would only take twenty minutes, maybe half an hour. She'd have plenty of time to go there, stay a while, then come back to join the audience again."

"Let me do the second interview with Corinne Jawalski," said Bourke. "I'll use my famous charm."

"Gosh," said Anne. "Can I watch?"

Carol was amused and pleased by this gentle mockery. She had always found the most effective teams had this combination of trust, good humor and, underneath it all, respect. "What else, Anne?"

Anne had gleaned no further information on whether anyone had tried to find out whether Raeburn's body had been brought to the morgue, but she had spent some time with the scene-of-crime fingerprint expert. Raeburn's fingerprints appeared in the appropriate places, including the whiskey bottle and the glass he had used. The pattern of prints on Raeburn's copy of *The Euthanasia Handbook,* however, was particularly interesting. His palm print appeared along the spine, as though he'd held it rather awkwardly in one hand and opened it with the other. His thumb print appeared on the page detailing the necessary drug dosages to cause death. Among several other smudged prints on the cover of the paperback, some were definitely identifiable as

Raeburn's. Anne said, "The book's quite new and looks as though it's hardly been touched. When he was reading it he must have turned each page by the very edge. If you try it yourself, I think you'll find most people turn over each page at the top right-hand corner, and leave at least partial prints on both sides."

Bourke yawned and stretched. "Think it could be a setup, Anne?"

"Maybe. Or Raeburn knew exactly which page he wanted, so he went straight to it and kept it open with his thumb while he read it."

"What do you think, Carol?"

"I don't think he bought the book and I don't think he read it. Of course, proving that's a little harder. Incidentally, have both of you read the handbook right through?" When they shook their heads, she said, "I haven't done anything other than glance at the relevant pages either, and there might be something we've missed."

"Oh good," said Bourke. "I need a little light reading."

"Anne," Carol said, "I don't suppose you've turned anything up on where the book was purchased?"

"It's negative for all the bookshops near the hotel, but if Raeburn had been planning this for some time he could have bought it anywhere."

"It may be necessary to cover the bookshops again with photographs of possible suspects. I think the book was a prop to add one more convincing touch to a suicide scenario."

"You really do think it's murder?" said Bourke.

"Sure of it."

"Told the Commissioner?"

Carol smiled wryly. "I've already told him I think murder's a possibility, but I'm damned sure he won't welcome anything more definite than that."

"Care to tell us why you're so certain?"

"Little things, but they add up. He didn't leave a note. The whole scene in the hotel room looked theatrical and staged. His daily journal's missing. He had a colossal ego that should reject suicide. The handbook looks like an obvious prop and the pattern of fingerprints on it seems odd. He sticks to his diet, even though it's going to be his last meal."

"And," said Bourke, "he wasn't universally loved by those who knew him well. In fact, he was pretty well hated." He started ticking the names off on his fingers. "Alanna Brooks is about to be supplanted by his latest love, Corinne Jawalski; Corinne herself is in conflict with him, but we don't know why; Lloyd Clancy's a rival tenor, and coming off second best in the career stakes; both Edward Livingston, as manager-producer, and Graeme Welton as composer, have a lot tied up in *Dingo*, but Raeburn was set to wreck everything by bailing out of his contract; Nicole Raeburn's a loony where her brother is concerned; Kenneth Raeburn's playing fast and loose with the family company." He sat back with an air of satisfaction. "There you are, Carol. At least seven people might have had an interest in terminating Collis Raeburn's illustrious career."

"The motives you give are enough to have someone think about killing him—but to actually do it asks for a lot more than dislike or even hatred. Raeburn's murder was carefully planned and just as carefully carried out. Whoever did it had a motivation much stronger than anything that's obvious so far."

"How about the AIDS angle?"

"You're right, Mark. It could be someone we haven't turned up yet ... or it could be a lover who Raeburn's infected."

Mark looked grim. "But why kill Raeburn so mercifully, Carol? If he's HIV-positive it's likely that he's doomed anyway ... as is the hypothetical lover. And even if Raeburn survives, and doesn't develop full-blown AIDS, he has all the mental torment of waiting to become terribly ill, not to mention what the publicity will do to his career."

"Yes," said Carol. "The publicity. I think that might be a key to whole thing."

The Commissioner's bass voice boomed in Carol's ear. "Nicole Raeburn's got to the Minister, and the Minister's got to me. Seems Ms Raeburn doesn't find you very cooperative, Carol."

"By that I think she means I didn't say what she wanted to hear."

"Any developments?"

"Only that I'm convinced it's homicide."

"Oh, shit," said the Commissioner.

On the telephone Kenneth Raeburn's soft voice sounded slyly intimate. "Inspector Ashton, I really would like to see you as soon as possible. I know it's

Saturday tomorrow, but I'll be in the city, so I wonder if we could have lunch?"

She had no intention of letting him have the advantage of choosing the venue for their meeting. "I'm sorry," she said crisply, "but I have very little time because of the investigation. If it's convenient, perhaps you could come here tomorrow afternoon. Would that be possible?"

As she put down the receiver she frowned. The Raeburns were using their clout to bring pressure to bear on her to get the result they wanted. But why? Was it simply because suicide was unacceptable, unthinkable? That they honestly believed he had accidentally killed himself?

Carol was well aware that the coroner would be willing to suppress Collis Raeburn's HIV status if her investigations indicated accidental death, but should her report canvass suicide or murder, then this embarrassing detail was very relevant and would be given full weight, with the attendant publicity.

She picked up the phone and punched in Bourke's extension. "Mark? I'm seeing Kenneth Raeburn tomorrow afternoon. Please apologize to Pat, so close to the wedding, but I'd like you to be there, and would you bring as much financial information on the Raeburn family company as you can get."

The wedding. Sybil will be there ... We can talk on neutral territory.

Carol had arranged to pick up Madeline Shipley at the television studio at seven-thirty after her program aired. She waited in the visitors' lounge with a mixture of anticipation and apprehension as if, for some reason she didn't understand, this meeting would be significant.

She tried to be objective when she saw Madeline approaching. She was slightly built, came only to Carol's shoulder, and moved with definitive grace. She was wearing her burnished hair loose and had replaced the heavy studio makeup with a trace of lipstick and eyeliner. She had deeply gray eyes, and a curved, sensual mouth.

"Carol!" she said, the charisma that had such potent force on a television screen muted, but still striking. "Shall we embrace, or would that be too confronting for a Detective Inspector?"

"Far too confronting," said Carol, matching her flippant tone. "Perhaps we should shake hands."

Madeline linked her arm through Carol's. "I'm absolutely starving. Don't try to get a word out of me until I've eaten."

In the car she lightly touched Carol's knee. "Hey, lighten up. Won't hurt you to relax and let down that formidable barrier you hide behind."

Carol, disconcerted by the ripple of sensation caused by Madeline's fingers, concentrated on her driving. After a moment she said, "Put your seatbelt on."

Madeline, curled up to sit sideways on the seat, snorted derisively. "I hate seatbelts."

Out of the corner of her eye Carol could see that she was smiling. Carol said, "Madeline, this is ridiculous. You're breaking the law."

"So what're you going to do, Officer? Arrest me?"

She chuckled. "You could handcuff me. That sounds promising."

Carol sighed. "Are you going to be in this mood all night?"

Madeline wriggled around to click on her seatbelt. Abruptly serious, she said, "What's wrong, Carol? Are things okay between you and Sybil?"

"Nothing's wrong."

"Forgive me. I shouldn't have asked that."

Her hand on Carol's shoulder had the same disconcerting effect as her earlier touch had had. Carol almost said, *Don't touch me.* She smiled as she considered what Madeline's response would be.

"Okay Carol, I've made you smile at last. What did I say, so I can do it again?"

"I was just thinking of something."

"That's your trouble—you think too much. Why don't you, just for once, take a chance? Do something outrageous?"

Carol turned smoothly into the restaurant carpark. "I may order dessert tonight," she said. "That outrageous enough?"

The restaurant had achieved the elusive mix of attentive service and circumspection. Carol and Madeline sat in a private island, attended by unobtrusive waiters and plied with expensive wine and exquisitely presented food.

"Looks far too good to eat," said Madeline as her order, cornets of trout, was placed in front of her. Carol smiled an agreement. Her own dish was flawless miniature vegetables grouped reverently around veal cutlets.

"It's the secret of my occasional culinary success,"

said Madeline. "I can't cook my way out of a predampened paper bag, but I can sure present things so they look good. And that fools people, you know. They think if it *looks* good, it must taste the same."

Over coffee, Carol said, "Okay, I've been patient." "Was Collis Raeburn HIV-positive?"

"Tell me why you think he might have been."

As Madeline smiled, Carol noticed that one of her teeth was slightly uneven. Somehow such imperfection in one of such polished comeliness was endearing.

"Carol, how do I know you'll give me an exclusive if I tell you what I know?"

"Trust me. And tell me anyway, because you'll be obstructing justice if you don't."

"I love it when you're tough."

"Madeline . . ."

"Okay, okay. The channel, or, more specifically, my program, was approached by a guy who claimed to have a story for sale about Collis Raeburn's HIV status. He'd obviously heard we were preparing a special and thought we might be in the market for some scandal, so he demanded twenty thousand for the story, fifty if we put him on camera."

Carol sat forward. "Who is he?"

"Says his name's Amos Berringer. Claims to be an ex-lover who's got the dirt on Raeburn's clandestine activities."

Wanting to appear casual, Carol leaned back in her chair. "Suppose you've checked him out?"

"Surely that's your job," said Madeline, grinning.

"So you're paying him twenty thousand on spec?"

"Of course not. We checked him out." She made a

face. "Grubby little number, who seems to have made some spare cash gently blackmailing married men who fancied a dabble in gay sex."

"I'll run him—see if we have anything on an Amos Berringer."

Madeline shrugged. "Doubt if you will. The word we have is that Berringer's careful of his marks. They're always the sort who'd pay rather than run any risk of publicity."

Carol felt somehow disappointed that Collis Raeburn would have anything to do with someone like Berringer. "Did he show you any hard evidence, or was it all colorful description?"

"He swears Collis Raeburn was HIV-positive and that he got it from unprotected gay sex." She paused to see if Carol would respond, then said, "Well? Was he a candidate for AIDS?"

Carol felt a thrill of anticipation. This was an approach to Raeburn from another angle, and information gained here might dovetail with other apparently unrelated pieces to form a coherent picture. She said matter-of-factly, "Just tell me what you've got."

Madeline opened her purse and handed Carol an envelope. "A brief report on Berringer and copies of a couple of photos he gave us. They're nothing startling, just Raeburn in what looks like a gay bar. Berringer's playing coy and won't say where it is, because, he says, he doesn't want anyone else selling us the story."

The photographs clearly identified Raeburn in a crowd of men, many dressed in leather and all apparently having a good time. He wore jeans and a denim shirt and was laughing in both photographs:

115

in one toasting a startlingly handsome young man; in the other apparently sharing a joke with a group notable for bare chests, leather and studs.

"Straights have been known to go to gay bars, just for the novelty," Carol said. Then, "I don't want you to run this story."

"It's too thin anyway, unless we get more from Berringer. Frankly, we're stringing him along so he doesn't offer it anywhere else, but if it looks like anyone in the media has it, we'll go to air straight away."

"Will you tell me if you're going to do that?"

Madeline smiled lazily. "For you, anything."

Half an hour later, walking back to the car, Madeline said, "Do I get an exclusive, now that I've cooperated so fulsomely with you?"

Carol looked at her sideways. "I won't promise anything. You know that."

"Ah," said Madeline with a soft laugh, "but you're full of infinite promise, Carol."

They were silent on the drive to Madeline's. Carol again felt the disturbing combination of anxiety and anticipation. She tried to rationalize it away—the anger and disappointment she felt about Sybil was fueling this disturbance to her usual equilibrium.

Madeline's house was set back from the road and extensively landscaped for privacy. Carol turned into the driveway and drew up smoothly at the shallow sandstone steps.

She said, her voice deliberately cool, "Good night . . . and thank you for the information."

"Would you like to come inside?"

"Thanks, but no. It's late."

"Since Paul's been gone . . . I've been lonely."

"It's not a good idea."

"Sure it is, Carol. You know it is."

"No, I don't know that at all."

"It's going to happen. Why not now?"

"Good night, Madeline."

Madeline slid out of the car and walked around to the driver's door. Carol wound the window down, looked up at her. "Madeline, we're not doing a reprise of *Desert Hearts* you know."

Madeline was smiling. She leaned through the window and kissed Carol lightly on the lips. Drawing back, she said cheerfully, "It's going to be fun, Carol. And more . . ."

Carol turned the ignition key. "No."

Her emphatic negative drew a broader smile from Madeline as she stood back from the car. "I can feel it, and so can you. Say what you like—it won't make any difference."

When Carol glanced in the rear view mirror as she turned out of the driveway, Madeline was still standing there, gazing after her. Carol swore, trying with words to chase away the spiraling tension that Madeline's words and touch had accomplished.

Carol was home before Sybil, who had a committee meeting for Women in Politics. The red light was blinking on the answering machine, so she pressed replay while she primed her ancient coffee percolator. The first message was from her Aunt Sarah, confirming her plans to arrive on Saturday morning. The second was a whispered voice she didn't recognize. *Collis Raeburn's death was an accident. Put that in your report. Just say he died accidentally. It's the best thing to do for everyone, and it's true. Don't cause trouble. There's some things about your private life you wouldn't want to get out. Remember that.*

She stood staring at the machine as it clicked loudly, then wound the tape back with an angry whirring sound. Carol pressed the replay button, listening intently as the whispered voice repeated the message. Blended with a brush of apprehension was anger—and the tingle of excitement that her investigation had driven someone to make the threat.

CHAPTER SEVEN

Collis Raeburn's singing teacher lived in an old suburb that had once enjoyed more gracious days. Her house, an undistinguished dark brick, sat stolidly in a neglected garden. Carol shivered as she got out of the car. The day had begun with icy wind and sudden, spiteful showers of rain, as a reminder that it was only very early spring.

Earlier, the sharpness of the day had been echoed by the coldness between her and Sybil. "Carol, there's been something wrong between us for a long time. I've grown, I've changed, and the way you want to live isn't enough for me anymore."

Restraining her anger, Carol had said, "Is running away the best thing to do?"

"We need to have some distance between us ... *I* need some distance ..."

"Don't do this, darling."

Sybil's face had tightened at this brisk entreaty. "Carol, we always do it *your* way—this time it's going to be different ..."

Anne Newsome broke into her somber thoughts. Gesturing at the house, she said, "Being a singing teacher doesn't seem very profitable. Must be in it for love."

Love? thought Carol bitterly.

As they opened the sagging gate and walked up the overgrown path, a voice, warm as sunshine, poured out the open window. The sung phrase curled in the air, then faded. A pause, and it was repeated.

Carol knocked sharply on the door. After a few moments it was opened by a woman whose face was familiar from the Collis Raeburn television special. "Inspector Ashton? You're a little early. I'm just finishing a lesson. Won't be long."

As they were shown into an alcove off the front room, Carol glimpsed the polished flank of a grand piano and the slight figure of a young woman standing beside it. She and Anne settled down into lumpily uncomfortable lounge chairs upholstered in dusty brocade.

The lesson recommenced. The young woman would sing a phrase, the dark liquid of her voice caressing the notes, only to be interrupted by an impatient comment and a command to do it again.

"No! No! Listen to yourself. Where's your control? Remember, your voice is supported by a column of air . . . Put your hands against your ribs, here, fingers touching . . . Now, breathe in! Let the air force your hands apart."

A pause, apparently for the student to comply. Anne caught Carol's glance and smiled. The teacher's impatient voice demanded, "You feel that? Do you? Do it again! . . . Now, you must always remember that the muscular arch of your diaphragm is the foundation of your voice. Singing is only air passing over your vocal cords, so you must control that column of air completely."

There was a soft comment from the student, followed by an impatient exclamation from the teacher. "Most people are lazy and breathe shallowly. *You* must learn to use every part of your lungs—they are the bellows of your voice." A chord was struck violently on the piano. "Don't sing the note—hum! Louder . . . *louder*. Now! Swell it . . . fade it. You feel your upper lip vibrating? Yes? Remember that feeling. That's where your voice must be placed to get that clear, beautiful, sustained sound."

"Seems like hard work," whispered Anne.

The teacher had begun a piano introduction. The music was unfamiliar to Carol, but it filled the room with an aching melody that intensified as the young woman began to sing. Her voice—tawny and supple—delighted Carol. She shut her eyes and let it curl around her. This time there were no interruptions. The song ended with a few soft notes, then the voice of the teacher saying grudgingly, "That was better. But you must practice. Practice!"

The lesson over, the student was bustled out the

front door and Carol and Anne were taken into the main room. "Your student's got a beautiful voice," said Anne.

The teacher grunted. "Oh, yes, God's given her the voice. But that's just the first step. It's what she does with it now, that's important. She could be the next Kathleen Ferrier—if she works hard, and gets the breaks. It's never enough to have raw talent. Luck has a lot to do with success."

"Collis Raeburn was lucky?" said Carol.

The woman's stern face softened. "Yes, Collis was lucky, but he also had a voice that only occurs once or twice a century. He was sent to me early, before he could learn shortcuts and bad habits—tenors often develop them, I'm afraid—and I realized immediately what he was." She grew grim. "That is all the more reason why it is a dreadful tragedy that he's dead."

"You said on the phone to me that you believed someone had killed him."

The teacher's eyes narrowed at Carol's bland tone. "I can see you doubt me, but I *know* someone did." She gave a theatrical shrug. "You'll be thinking I'm overdramatizing, no doubt. But I knew Collis better than anyone, and there is no way he would have killed himself. He had an arrogance, bordering on narcissism, that would make it absolutely impossible for him to even consider destroying himself. Suicide, no matter what, could not be an option."

Carol said mildly, "Just hypothetically, what if he'd been suffering from something like cancer..."

"You don't have to pussyfoot around. I knew about the AIDS."

Hiding her surprise, Carol said, "What did he tell you, and when?"

"About a week before he died he came to see me here. Said he'd tested positive. He was angry and upset, but he wasn't about to kill himself over it. Collis was a fighter. Wouldn't have got where he did in his career if he was the sort to throw up his hands and give up. He told me he was determined to beat the virus. That he could afford the best advice, the latest drugs . . . and he firmly believed a cure was probable within the next few years."

Carol said bluntly, "Did he have any idea how he caught it?"

She glared. "All he said was it was someone he knew. Said he'd get even, any way he could."

"Any idea if it was a man or woman? Did he give a name?"

"No. And I didn't ask, Inspector." Her face contorted with grief and anger. "Wish I had, because whoever it was killed him to keep him quiet. I'm sure of it."

As Anne drove them back into the city, she said rather smugly to Carol, "I think I know why he told the housekeeper and his singing teacher, but no one else."

"He may have told several people, but they're not saying anything." Anne looked subdued by this comment, so Carol prompted, "What's your theory?"

"Well, since Collis Raeburn's mother died when he was very young, and the housekeeper and his singing teacher are sort of middle-aged, I think they might be mother-substitutes for him." She flushed slightly. "That's just off the top of my head."

"It's an interesting point, Anne. And it could lead somewhere, or not, but it's worth saying."

After an awkward pause, Carol said, "Who was Kathleen Ferrier?"

Anne grinned. "Luckily I can answer that, because my father had all her records. She was an English contralto with the most beautiful voice. She died young from cancer, and her records are all mono recordings, but they're still wonderful."

Singers live on in their recordings, thought Carol. *What will I leave behind?*

Back in her office, Carol closed the door and dialed home. "Sybil? Have you changed your mind?... Darling, please..." She listened, her face blank, then said, "Are you taking Jeffrey with you?"

Ridiculously, the mention of Sybil's fat ginger cat brought her closest to tears. She blinked, keeping her voice steady as she said, "I'm glad you're leaving him with me. Sinker would be lonely without his company—"

A sharp knock at the door interrupted, but she knew Sybil wanted to end the call anyway. They'd said everything that could be said last night. Her voice still calm, with no hint of the gray desolation that filled her, she said goodbye and replaced the receiver deliberately.

Bourke opened the door. "Carol, sorry to interrupt, but I've seen Amos Berringer, the would-be exposé king."

She gestured for him to sit, resolutely pushing

her despair about Sybil out of her mind. "Was he selling a genuine story?"

"Not really. He's a sleazy little bastard, skating around the edges of the gay scene and picking up married guys cruising for a quick thrill. His m.o. is to take a photograph or two on the sly, then try a little blackmail for, as he calls it, gifts. Seems the photos of Raeburn were pure luck—he recognized him in the bar and decided to take a few snaps for future reference. He's dropped the claim he was Raeburn's ex-lover, and now says he just moved in the same crowd."

"So why the story that Raeburn was HIV-positive? How could he have known he was?"

Bourke shrugged. "It might just be Berringer's lucky guess. He probably thought, too, that it would make a stronger story for sale to Madeline Shipley."

Carol was finding it an effort to concentrate. Forcing her thoughts away from Sybil's angry words—"Everything's got to be on *your* terms, Carol. Everything."—she asked if Bourke had traced anyone else in the photographs.

"Not yet, but we've got the name of the bar and I've got Ferguson chasing up any names we got from Berringer." He paused, irresolute, then said, "Remember you asked me to pick up on what was being said on the grapevine? You won't like it, Berringer but the general impression seems to be that you're in the Commissioner's pocket on this one and the result—accidental death—is a foregone conclusion. Bannister, of course, is helping this along, although I've managed to point out to a few people it's sour grapes on his part."

"There was a call on my answering machine last night—no name, of course—advising me to find that Raeburn's death was an accident. It was whispered, but possibly a man." She couldn't bring herself to mention the threat of exposure. She didn't want Mark Bourke's sympathy, or his understanding. *I can pretend it hasn't happened—but that won't make it go away.*

Mark said dryly, "It'd be a lot less trouble if it *was* an accident."

She nodded wearily as her phone rang. "It sure would." Hoping it was Sybil calling back, she snatched up the receiver.

"Inspector Ashton? This is Alanna Brooks."

"I would like to see you as soon as possible."

"And I you, Inspector, but unfortunately it's the opening night of *Aida,* and, having missed so much yesterday, I'm tied up with rehearsals almost right through. I do, however, have a suggestion I hope you might accept. I've two tickets for one of the boxes, and I'd be delighted if you saw the performance tonight, then joined me in my dressing room afterwards. I'd be more than pleased to answer all your questions then."

Carol thought of her house, lonely without Sybil, and accepted the invitation.

The wind had dropped, so the night was cool, not cold. The Opera House looked its spectacular best. The patrician curves of the floodlit cream-tiled roof shells were a counterpoint to the dark heaving water of the harbor, the ribs of the Harbour Bridge and the garish vitality of the city.

Carol met Anne Newsome in the foyer. The stark concrete curved in buttresses to support the soaring roofs, the walls were curtains of glass that allowed the city's changing pattern of lights to provide a background to the crowds thronging around the circular central bars.

Mark Bourke had reacted with horror at the idea of attending an opera, but Anne had been delighted. "I know you don't have to really dress up for opening nights anymore," she had said, "but it's a great chance to get your glad rags out!"

Aware that she would be interviewing Alanna Brooks, and, as always, wanting to create a controlled impression, Carol had selected a severe black dress and discreet gold earrings. Anne had been rather more daring. Looking impossibly glamorous, in comparison to her working garb of plain, serviceable clothes, Anne was a vision in metallic green. "Startling, eh?" she said, as Carol blinked.

"Arresting," said Carol, her lips twitching.

Douglas Binns had been waiting anxiously for them. "Inspector! Please come this way. Miss Brooks has asked that you be given some refreshments before the performance begins."

Carol sipped her glass of champagne and considered Binns over the rim. "Mr. Binns, I presume you'd know everything that goes on in the opera company?"

He made haste to deny this. "By no means, Inspector. You must remember, I work for the Opera

House itself. The Eureka Company is here for a season only."

Giving him her most charming smile, Carol said, "Nevertheless, I would like you to answer a few questions." Before he could voice his protest, she went on, "And I do appreciate your position, Mr. Binns."

"Well, of course, if I can be of any help ..."

She asked a few mild questions about his work responsibilities, then, when he had relaxed, she said, "You're in a unique position, Mr. Binns, to give me unbiased information about the interrelationships in the Eureka Opera Company."

"I don't listen to gossip," he assured her quickly.

"It's not gossip I'm interested in, but your personal impressions. And of course, anything you say will be treated in confidence." He looked both flattered and wary as she went on, "As an outsider I'm at a disadvantage, so I need the insights you can give me."

She thought, *Have I laid it on too thick?* but was reassured by Douglas Binns's proud little smile.

"Well, yes, Inspector, of necessity I must know what's going on ..."

It was easy after that. He freely discussed the complicated web of allegiances, alliances, rivalries and open conflicts that, he assured Carol, characterized most artistic communities. He answered her specific questions about Collis Raeburn's relationships with a frankness that seemed to surprise him. "Inspector, I hope you don't think I discuss these matters on any other occasions. Even my wife doesn't know these details ..."

Bells rang to indicate that *Aida* would soon commence and in obedience to their gentle insistence, people began to straggle towards the entrances to the opera hall.

Binns was obviously rather taken with Anne in her metallic green dress. "Almost fifteen hundred and fifty seats," he said to her as he led them into their box high on the dull black left wall.

Out of habit Carol surveyed her surroundings carefully. A swelling murmur filled the opera theater as people crowded in, their animated conversations competing with discordant sounds from the cramped pit as the orchestra tuned up. Red seats with armrests in the familiar blond wood rose in tiers with no central aisle, so those in the center had to shuffle sideways past patrons already seated. The lighting was subdued, the banks of floodlights dark as they stared blankly at the heavy curtain masking the stage.

Binns was gazing around with proprietary pride. "Acoustics in the opera hall are very satisfactory," he said. "One point four reverb time!" He looked from Carol to Anne, as though expecting an admiring response. "You know, of course, that the singers use no electronic amplification."

"Why doesn't the orchestra drown them out?"

Anne's question pleased him. "I imagine," he said with a faintly superior smile, "that most—if not all—popular singing is very much the product of microphones and sound engineers, so that even a thin voice can be given weight and timbre electronically. This is not the case in grand opera. The voice is an instrument, and the singer must provide the controlled power and resonance to be in partnership with the orchestra, and often to soar above it."

Anne looked impressed. "They don't only have to compete with an orchestra, they have to act and sing in a foreign language, all at the same time. What happens if they get confused?"

Binns was clearly delighted with her appreciation of the rigors of opera. "Singers do have a little help," he said. "When the curtain goes up, you'll notice a little hood center stage front. It hides the prompt, who sits suspended over part of the orchestra pit in a space so small it's like sitting in a racing car."

The flutter of programs and the hum of voices stilled as the conductor entered. He acknowledged the applause, then turned to the orchestra. As the soft violins that introduced the prelude continued to soar above the threatening bass line, Carol consciously relaxed the tight muscles in her shoulders, determined to escape into the music.

The curtain slowly rose to show a vast columned hall with pyramids and temples in the background. Spontaneous applause broke out at the designer's achievement and at the hypnotically splendid Egyptian costumes. Carol was fascinated to see Lloyd Clancy stride to center stage. Gone was the cultured rogue with the ready smile and the wry humor she had encountered in the dressing room. He had been transformed into a young soldier, Radames, chosen by the goddess Isis to lead the Egyptian armies to victory against the Ethiopians. He sang with youthful joy the meltingly gorgeous "Celeste Aida." Carol found herself holding her breath. "Wow," said

Anne beside her as the last notes died to a rumble of applause.

A subtly glowing strip above the stage contained the subtitles, a continuous translation of the Italian into English as phrases were sung. *"Ritorna vincitor!"* sang the chorus with thrilling force: "So conquer and return!" the subtitles declared. At first Carol found the continuous translation distracting, but soon she seemed to absorb the words automatically, so that it was almost as if she understood Italian.

Initially Carol thought Alanna Brooks too mature and heavily built for the role of the young Aida, but the moment she began to sing, her voice, pure and piercingly beautiful, overrode this impression. She *was* Aida, daughter of the king of Ethiopia, sold into slavery to the pharaoh's daughter, Amneris, who loved, as did Aida, the young soldier, Radames.

After the Grand March an overwhelming mass of choral sound arose as the solo singers strove to be heard above the chanting of the priests, the cries of the captives and the shouts of the crowd. The descent of the curtain and the buzz from the audience as the lights came up for an interval was an unwelcome intrusion into the intoxicating world that the opera had created.

Resenting the return of reality, Carol remained almost silent, as Binns and Anne chatted about the gratifying fact that, for once, Edward Livingston had not tried to modernize or change the opera. As she sipped the champagne Binns had provided with somewhat self-satisfied facility, Carol wondered if the love triangle in *Aida* had disturbing parallels with her own life. Unwillingly she thought of Madeline

131

and Sybil as two points of a triangle of which she was the third. But wasn't she just romanticizing what was merely a disconcerting physical response to Madeline Shipley? Her thoughts moved on to the investigation. Had Collis Raeburn been one point in a romantic triangle? Was the key to his death held by a jealous lover?

As the third act began, Carol was preoccupied with the motives that might lie behind Collis Raeburn's death. Who, male or female, had loved, and then hated him enough to murder him? A sudden thought intruded: could he have actually killed himself in remorse for unknowingly infecting someone he loved with AIDS?

She was swept back into the music. In the moonlight on the banks of the Nile by the Temple of Isis, Alanna Brooks began to sing an exquisite lament. "Oh native skies ... never shall I see thee more," declared the subtitles. Carol shut her eyes, surrendering to the sensuous beauty of the melody.

Later, following Binns through the warren of corridors with Anne, the magical world created by the performance was dissipated. Robed priests, who a few minutes before had been singing sonorous condemnations as they lowered the slab of stone that would forever entomb Radames and Aida, were now a motley crowd engaged in mundane conversation as they made their way back to the dressing rooms.

The cream-colored door to Alanna Brooks's dressing room was open, with noise and people spilling out into the wide corridor. Binns efficiently, and officiously, shepherded everyone out, and then ushered Carol and Anne in.

The earlier meeting had been so brief that Carol had formed only a faint impression of Alanna Brooks, so she was fascinated to meet her now, particularly after seeing the ravishing performance she had given in the opera.

The diva sat at a mirror taking off her makeup. Seen close up, the illusion created on the stage dissolved. Shorter than Carol had remembered, she was big-busted and a little thick around the waistline. Her hair was reddish-brown and her skin pale and lightly freckled. Although laughter lines fanned from the corners of her eyes and her skin had coarsened a little, she had an amused confidence that made her seem much younger. "Inspector Ashton. At last! I'm so sorry to have been so difficult about this interview."

Carol was struck by the dark, husky timbre of her voice. Obviously Anne was too, as she said to Alanna, "You have a deep voice..."

"And I sing so high." She smiled warmly. "People often mention that. Speaking voices don't always indicate a singer's range. I started as a mezzo-soprano, and then, with training, extended my upper register. It's not that unusual—Joan Sutherland wasn't a soprano to begin with, either."

Carol wanted to get down to business. She

glanced at Anne, who took out her notebook. After refusing a drink, Carol made the appropriate compliments about the opera, then said directly, "Can you tell me anything about Mr. Raeburn's death?"

"Poor Collis. That was a dreadful thing for him to do."

"Did you have any suspicion he might suicide? Did he say or do anything in the days before it happened?"

Alanna had turned back to the mirror and was creaming her face. "No more than usual. Collis was always moody." She turned to smile at Carol. "We opera singers are all a little crazy, you understand. We spend our working time plotting, killing, being raped, deserted, murdered and/or suffering the pangs of unrequited love, so is it any wonder we're unbalanced at times?"

Carol didn't return her smile. "Are you saying Mr. Raeburn was unbalanced?"

Her smile vanished. "Of course I'm not!" A pause, then, "Well, he must have been ... to do that."

"You're assuming it was suicide."

Alanna stared at her. "Wasn't it?"

Carol said, "We don't know ... yet."

"Kenneth Raeburn assures me it was an accident. He's persuaded you of that too, has he?"

The hint of contempt in Alanna's voice stung, but Carol merely said, "I didn't realize you and Collis Raeburn's father were friends."

"Friends? Hardly, Inspector. He wanted Collis to ditch me for Corinne, and he was furious when Collis wouldn't."

"Ms Jawalski gave me the impression that she was sure she was going to replace you."

Alanna threw back her head and laughed. "Gorgeous voice and a brain like a split pea—that's our Corinne!"

Her amusement seemed quite genuine. Carol said, "Might it be possible that Mr. Raeburn was telling you one story and Corinne Jawalski another?"

Still smiling, Alanna said, "No. I'd had it out with Collis and he'd agreed to ring Corinne and tell her she had no hope of replacing me." Carol's skeptical expression made her add, "I knew Collis very well, Inspector. When he said he would do something, he did." She smiled wryly. "Of course, the trick was to get him to commit himself. He could be slippery as an eel, but once he'd promised, he'd carry it through."

"You knew him when you were both starting your careers."

Carol's statement brought a sudden stillness. "We knew each other when we were young." She smiled in self-derision. "He was rather younger than me, actually."

"You were lovers?"

Alanna Brooks cocked her head. "Just what are you getting at, Inspector? That's old news. I hate to tell you how many years ago it was."

"I've been told that rather recently you renewed the relationship."

The diva made a derisive sound. "Sure, for publicity reasons. It always titillates the public to think we might be lovers off-stage as well as on. There was nothing in it at all. We both hammed it

135

up for the media, not that they took that much notice, anyway."

"So," said Carol, "if your leading man had been Lloyd Clancy instead of Collis Raeburn, you would have been quite happy to play lovers for publicity with him?"

Alanna took a deep breath. "Not Lloyd Clancy, no."

"What would be the difference? Publicity is publicity."

"This doesn't seem at all relevant."

Carol let the steel show. "I'll decide that, Ms Brooks. Am I to take it that you don't like Lloyd Clancy?"

"Like him? I despise him." She put up a hand. "All right, you're going to ask me why. It's a personality clash, nothing more than that." Carol waited. Alanna went on reluctantly, her pale skin flushed, "I can see I'll have to be frank, although it's embarrassing for me. The fact is, I took a romantic interest in Lloyd that he didn't return. He was quite brutal about it and . . ." She shrugged. "There you have it."

Carol asked a few more questions about the relationship which Alanna parried with increasing composure. Carol said, "Have you read *The Euthanasia Handbook?*"

"No, but I was with Collis when he bought a copy."

Anne's head came up. Carol said, "When would that be?"

"About two weeks ago, I think. We were shopping

together in the city and we went into several bookshops. I'm not sure which one it was, but Collis bought a copy. He said he was interested because of the court case."

"Have you read it?"

Alanna looked puzzled. "Me? Of course not. Why would I be interested?" Her expression changed. "It's strange, but Kenneth Raeburn asked me the same thing."

"Why was that?"

"He came to see me before the performance tonight." She moved her shoulders irritably. "Can't stand the way he whispers, can you?"

Carol smiled faintly at this attempt to find common ground and so forge an ephemeral friendship, a tack familiar from many interviews. "Go on," she said.

"He told me it was becoming quite clear that Collis had accidentally killed himself, but the fact that there was a copy of the handbook in the room was a problem. Asked me if I'd read it, and when I asked why, he said he thought it might have been mine, and I'd lent it to Collis to read."

"Do you think he really meant that?"

"No," said Alanna decisively, "he was telling me indirectly that he wanted me to say it was my book, Collis hadn't gone out and bought it for himself. You see, Inspector, as soon as he'd made the comment, he began to talk about my career—how it could be helped or hindered."

Carol was intrigued. "What did you read into that?"

"Why," said Alanna, "that he was telling me if I cooperated it would be to my advantage, and if I didn't, I'd be very sorry."

"Did you take it seriously?"

"Of course," said Alanna. "Kenneth Raeburn loves to pull strings ... it's Napoleonic, I think. If he'd been born taller, it'd have been easier for everyone."

CHAPTER EIGHT

Saturday morning was deceptively sunny, the brisk wind having enough bite to be unpleasant. Carol had got up early, gone for a run with Olga, her neighbor's German shepherd, and come back to breakfast and *The Euthanasia Handbook*. She had just finished it when a car horn indicated Justin had arrived. Carol had always hated the way he'd sit in his car and imperiously summon people with long blasts from the horn. Swearing to herself, she put down the book and strode outside. David and Aunt

Sarah had arrived at almost the same time, David leaping out of his father's Mercedes, Aunt Sarah scrambling from a taxi.

As Carol saw her son, she was filled with an intensity of love that was almost terrifying. Away from him, thinking of him, made her gentle with affection, but when she actually saw David, she was always aware that she had no control over her feelings, and that she could—and would—sacrifice anything for him.

She hugged him and Aunt Sarah, gave the requisite wishes for a good trip to Justin and Eleanor, who were running late and so did not linger, and took her son and aunt inside out of the wind. David immediately went out onto the huge back deck to annoy Sinker and Jeffrey, who had found the only sunny sheltered spots available and were snoozing.

"Where's Sybil?" asked Aunt Sarah, taking off a red cardigan to reveal a blindingly bright purple top.

Carol felt her throat tighten. She said unemotionally, "She moved back to her house. I would have called you, but I thought it was better to tell you in person."

Aunt Sarah, short, plump and formidably energetic, snatched up the two fat bags she had insisted on carrying into the house. "Right, Carol. I'll put these in my room while you make me a cup of tea—you've neglected to offer it, I might mention—and you can tell me all about it."

Carol watched her aunt stride down the hall, her short white hair standing on end from the wind.

With her tanned, wrinkled face and its mobile expressions, she was a beloved if sometimes exasperating person who had more affectionate power over Carol than she cared to permit to anyone else.

Carol had just finished pouring the mugs of tea when her aunt reappeared. "Before David comes in from teasing the cats—he shouldn't be allowed to do that—you'd better tell me all about it." She glared. "Don't sigh, Carol. Just talk."

Feeling uncertain how to broach the subject, Carol said, "Aunt, I've never spelled it out, but Sybil and I . . ."

"Are lovers. Or is it *were* lovers?"

She winced. "Are, I think. I'm not sure."

Her aunt stirred sugar into her tea as though punishing the beverage. "Not like you to be unsure. If there's one thing you are, my dear, it's definite."

She realized what an enormous relief it was to share this part of herself with someone she trusted, whose love was secure. "Sybil says we've grown apart. That I won't keep up with her, won't try. She wants me to change—and I can't." She could hear the echo of resentment in her voice.

Aunt Sarah marched over to the sliding door. "David, cats don't want to play when they're trying to sleep. That's teasing. Don't let me see you do it again." Back at the kitchen bench, she said, "Is there someone else?"

"No, it's nothing like that."

"Your work has a lot to do with it," said Aunt Sarah shrewdly.

Carol told her about the wedding invitation. "It

only precipitated it, of course. Sybil won't accept that I have to stay in the closet. It isn't a matter of choice. If I want to do my job well, that's just one of the ground rules."

"Where's Sybil?" asked David, coming into the room with a blast of cold air.

Carol felt herself softening as she looked at him. He had her fair hair and green eyes, but his father's sturdy build. "She staying down at her house at the beach. When I spoke to her this morning she asked you and Aunt Sarah to go down for lunch. I have to go in to work, but I'll drive you down and pick you up later this afternoon."

"Can I go swimming?"

"Of course not," said Aunt Sarah. "It's far too cold. But we can try fishing, if you like. Have you got a line for me?" As David went off to find the fishing tackle he always left at Carol's place, she said, "Carol, don't take this so seriously. I left your uncle at least three times."

"You're making that up."

Aunt Sarah frowned. "Are you calling your closest relative a liar?"

"I wouldn't dare," said Carol, grinning.

Sybil looked relaxed in a black track suit that emphasized the red of her hair. She welcomed David and Aunt Sarah with warmth, Carol with more restraint.

"I've told Aunt Sarah the situation."

Sybil said with certainty, "She won't take sides, Carol."

142

Carol was immediately indignant. "I wouldn't ask her to."

Driving into the city, she wondered if that was true. What would she feel if her aunt said to her that Sybil was right, and that Carol must change? Thought was unprofitable—she felt baffled and angry. She walked into her office with a feeling of relief that she could slip into the role she played best.

Mark Bourke had just come into her office when the phone rang to announce that Kenneth Raeburn was waiting to see her.

He entered full of soft smiles. "Inspector Ashton, I do appreciate you seeing me."

Introducing him to Bourke, she was again reminded of an aggressive bantam rooster. Bourke was much taller and more substantial, so Raeburn swelled his chest, stood almost on tiptoes, shook hands emphatically, then stepped away so that the height difference was not so obvious. "You'd like me to sit here, Inspector?"

Carol waited until both men were seated, then said, "I interviewed Alanna Brooks last night."

"A very fine soprano. Collis thought the world of her."

"She says she believes you were trying to persuade her to say that the book on euthanasia in the hotel room actually belongs to her. That it wasn't your son's at all."

He was dressed in a dark blue suit and red tie. He picked an imaginary speck from the lapel as he said, "Alanna, of course, is mistaken. I didn't try to persuade her of anything at all. We did, however, mention the handbook."

"You saw her just before the performance of *Aida*."

"Yes?" His tone was polite.

"It was opening night, so hardly the time for an informal chat. Why did you want to see her?"

His soft voice became hostile. "I can't imagine what this has to do with your investigation, but if you must know, I wanted her to tell me how Collis was when she last saw him."

Carol glanced at Bourke, who said, "It's almost a week since your son died, yet this is the first time you speak to Alanna Brooks?"

"Well, no. She rang me to offer her condolences earlier, but I felt I needed to see her face-to-face."

Bourke was unimpressed. "It wasn't a very convenient time, just before a major performance."

Raeburn reddened. "My son is dead! Whether it's convenient or inconvenient is of no interest to me."

It was Carol's turn. "Were Collis and Alanna Brooks lovers?"

"Years ago, when they were starting out—yes. But never after that. Besides, Collis was interested in Corinne Jawalski." Anticipating the next question, he said so softly that Carol had to listen intently, "I don't know if they were lovers. You'll have to ask Corinne."

"Ms Brooks says that you favored Corinne as a singing partner for your son."

"This is of no importance now, but I was looking to the future. I believe Corinne will reach the very top."

Bourke opened a folder. "Edward Livingston told us Alanna Brooks was a bankable star who could be guaranteed to pull the fans. Considering the

144

financial state of your family company, wouldn't it be wiser to stay with the tried and true?"

Raeburn seemed to be expanding with arrogant anger. His neck bulged over his tight white collar. "What have you got there? What have you been prying into?"

Bourke passed him the papers without a word.

Raeburn leafed through them, then said, "All right. There's a temporary cash flow problem. Nothing to worry about, as it's only short-term."

Pursing his lips, Bourke said, "Your son know about it? Could have preyed on his mind if he did..."

"He wasn't interested in the financial side of things. Left everything to me. As I said, it was a short-term problem anyway."

"I've had an accountant look these papers over," said Bourke cheerfully. "Says you were up the creek without a paddle..."

Madeline called as Carol and Bourke were reviewing the case. "Carol, could you drop in on your way home? Something's happened you should know."

"Can you tell me on the telephone?"

"No, I can't. I'll be here all afternoon, so call by any time."

"Madeline Shipley," said Carol in explanation as she replaced the receiver. "I'll call you if she's got anything important."

"We've still got nothing on the photo, but it's Saturday night when the boys come out to play, so I've got a couple of men checking the bars in Oxford

Street." He grinned. "Not being sexist, Carol, but this *is* a man's job."

Carol leaned her chin on her hands. "Okay, let's get this over and done with, and we can both go home."

He passed her a neatly ruled sheet. "Time of death is so vague that it seems almost any of his nearest and dearest could have helped him on his way, not to mention his enemies." They went down the list together, stopping to discuss each one.

Kenneth and Nicole Raeburn had agreed that they were both at home most of Saturday and Sunday. "They'd alibi each other, anyway," said Bourke, "so that means very little."

"Motives?"

"Kenneth Raeburn's in real financial trouble, and rumors persist that his son was about to dump him, audit the company and then bring in a professional manager. A verdict of accidental death will get him Collis's eight hundred thousand insurance, the embarrassment of HIV hushed up and the company assets to play with." He made a face. "As for his sister, strikes me she's nuts about her brother, in more ways than one. Still, the way he died seems too disciplined for her—she's the sort who'd lose her marbles, shove him off a building and then say, Ooops, he slipped . . ."

Corinne Jawalski had claimed to be at the Town Hall in the audience for *Elijah,* although, as Anne Newsome had pointed out, she had plenty of time to go to Collis Raeburn's room and then return before the end of the oratorio.

"How about bitter pique for a motive?" said Bourke. "She thinks she's got head diva sewn up,

146

then he reneges and says he's staying with Alanna and it's just too bad for her."

"Doesn't seem enough motive for a murder."

"How about," said Bourke grimly, "he infected her with AIDS? Wouldn't that be a reason to kill him?"

Graeme Welton was working alone all weekend on final touches to *Dingo* and had ignored phone calls, so he had no alibi. Bourke was jocular. "Welton's a friend of Nicole's, though God knows what's in it for him. Maybe he killed her brother on her behalf to save daddy's bacon, as well as to punish Collis for saying his new opera was going to go belly up."

His smile faded when Carol said, "He had a sexual relationship with Raeburn, and we don't know what his HIV status is . . ."

On Saturday night Edward Livingston had been at the Opera House gladhanding a group of society matrons who formed the influential fund-raising committee of a national charity. The cocktail party had ended with a harpsichord recital starting at eight in the tiny Playhouse Theater. "Livingston would have had no probs," said Bourke. "He could have slipped out, walked to the hotel, dealt with Raeburn, then been back in time to smile at the ladies as they trotted off into the night."

"And he might want Collis dead because he was about to lose him. Even if Livingston held him to his contract, there'd be a debilitating legal battle, expensive and embarrassing."

Both Alanna Brooks and Lloyd Clancy had been guests at a function honoring an ancient but still prolific artist at the Museum of Modern Art at the Rocks, which was very close to Raeburn's hotel. "Pat was there, too," said Bourke, "and she remembers speaking to both of them at different times, but she's vague about when. People came and went from seven-thirty on, and it was very crowded. Didn't end until well after eleven, and I'm still chasing up a guest list to see if I can get anything more concrete."

"All right, Mark—Alanna Brooks kills him because she's about to be supplanted as prima donna . . . and maybe there's a love triangle there too, with either Corinne Jawalski or Graeme Welton at the other point."

Bourke yawned. "Sorry Carol, had a late night—we went through the wedding rehearsal a hundred times, it seems. Now, who's left? Lloyd Clancy and Mr. X." He yawned again. "Clancy has a motive because Raeburn's career was eclipsing his. Something like that wouldn't worry me, but then, I'm not an opera singer."

"A mercy," said Carol.

"Cheer up," said Bourke, "if none of these motives attract you, there's always Mr. X—the guy Raeburn told his singing teacher he'd get even with. Maybe Mr. X got in first."

Carol frowned. "Doesn't have to be a Mr. X who infected him," she said. "Could be a woman."

Madeline, wearing a russet shirt, tight white jeans and an incandescent smile, opened the door. Carol said, "I've got to pick up David and my Aunt Sarah from Sybil's house, so I can only stay a few moments."

She had deliberately dropped the clue, and Madeline immediately picked it up. "At Sybil's house? Has she left you, Carol? Or did you throw her out?" Then, immediately contrite, "I shouldn't have said that."

"Why did you want to see me?"

Madeline seemed chilled by Carol's tone. "Are you coming inside? Please . . ."

Carol followed her down the short hall to a charmingly furnished sitting room with plate glass windows opening onto a landscaped garden. Stingingly conscious of Madeline's physical presence and of her heavy musk perfume, torn by fresh anguish over Sybil, Carol gazed resolutely at the greenery tossed by the wind.

"Amos Berringer's disappeared."

Carol looked at her. "Something's happened to him?"

"No. He's gone to ground. I think he's been paid off to keep him quiet."

"Any ideas?"

Madeline's heavy copper hair shone as she shook her head. "Thought your people'd be able to turn up something. I suspect it might be the father trying to hush things up, but then again, Collis could have been moving with some pretty heavy characters we know nothing about." She took a leather folder from a side table. "These are statements, notes, the report from a private detective we had check Berringer out—everything we collected." She gave a small smile. "I'm cooperating with the police, Carol. Won't you cooperate with me?"

"In what way?"

"Have you and Sybil separated?"

Carol stood. "This isn't a topic for discussion."

"It's important to me."

"Why?"

"You know why, Carol."

Checking her watch, Carol said, "I have to go."

Madeline laughed as though she'd won a victory. "Go," she said.

When Carol, David and Aunt Sarah came back from Sybil's, darkness was falling. While Aunt Sarah organized David into a bath before dinner, Carol listened to the one message on the answering machine.

The same whispered voice as before admonished her: *You haven't been paying attention, Carol Ashton. It was an accidental overdose. Why not just say that or do you want everyone to know what you and Sybil Quade do in bed? Collis Raeburn's death was an accident. Make sure your report says that.*

Sounds of enthusiastic splashing from the bathroom preceded Aunt Sarah, who came hurrying back into the kitchen area. "Who was that?"

Her aunt always moved with unsettling energy, towing less enthusiastic people along in her wake. She also had a tenacity that made prevarication pointless. Carol was horrified to hear a shake in her voice as she said, "It's just a rather well-mannered anonymous call trying to persuade me that Collis Raeburn accidentally killed himself."

Aunt Sarah squeezed her hand in unspoken

comfort, obviously realizing that Carol was struggling for control. She said prosaically, "Why well-mannered?"

It helped to be objective. "Anonymity often encourages people to swear, describe in graphic detail violence or sex ... this one's polite to an extraordinary extent, considering that he, or she, is threatening me."

Aunt Sarah looked alarmed. "Threatening you with what? Physical harm?"

It was hard to say the words. "Just exposure as a lesbian, Aunt. Just that."

"What are you going to do?"

"Wait," said Carol with bitter resignation. "There isn't anything else I can do. It may come to nothing. If not ... I'll worry about that if it happens."

If it happens? What about my career? And Sybil—have I sacrificed our relationship for an illusion of safety?

Aunt Sarah swooped on the electric kettle. "Tea, Carol. You've got to stop drinking coffee—I've told you what it does to you, so why do you persist?"

"I'm incorrigible?"

Abruptly serious, Aunt Sarah put her hand on Carol's arm. "Carol, I love you. I want you to remember you can talk to me about anything. You know that, don't you?"

Resigned, Carol said, "Has being with Sybil brought this on?"

"No, although she did talk to me about you."

"Oh, great!"

Aunt Sarah pursed her lips. "You don't really

communicate, Carol, that's the problem. How does anyone know what you're thinking and feeling behind that cool exterior of yours?"

"You don't seem to have any trouble."

Aunt Sarah grinned at the resentment in Carol's voice. "I've known you since you were a baby, that's why," she said with a hint of complacency. "You've always been as transparent as glass to me."

She handed Carol a mug of tea. "And don't ask for sugar. It isn't good for you."

"I don't take sugar."

"Good thing, too."

Carol ran her finger around the rim of the mug. "Aunt Sarah, what do I tell David?"

Her aunt didn't dissemble. "Tell him the truth."

Carol sighed. "Justin's pressuring me. Says David has to know about me and Sybil, about what I am."

Showing both impatience and concern, Aunt Sarah said, "What you are, my dear, is very important to him. You're his mother and his friend and he trusts and loves you. Tell him what he needs to know—no more and no less."

"How much is that?"

Aunt Sarah threw up her hands. "I don't know. How can there be a hard and fast rule? You'll have to play it by ear, Carol. There isn't any other way."

Sipping her tea, Carol thought, *Do I really need to say anything, now that Sybil's gone?* She was immediately ashamed. *Coward*, she accused.

CHAPTER NINE

Corinne Jawalski was not impressed by an early
Sunday morning visit from Carol. She yawned as she
pushed the heavy brown hair back from her face. "I
was hoping to sleep in. I've had a very heavy week."

"There's one little matter I'd like to clear up."

"Oh, yes?" said Corinne, unimpressed.

Carol looked around the apartment. The flatmate
was nowhere to be seen, but piles of magazines,
empty bottles, and one high-heeled shoe next to a
saucer with several lipstick-stained butts indicated
her presence.

"No, I don't smoke," said Corinne, following her glance. "And I've told Beth not to, but she's too selfish to stop."

"May I sit down?" asked Carol, convinced that it would be pointless to wait for ordinary courtesies from her.

Corinne nodded ungraciously. "All right, but you won't be long, will you?" She began to pace impatiently.

"I imagine you were angry after Collis Raeburn's call on Saturday night," said Carol conversationally.

A shrug. "Nothing to be angry about."

"He told you that Alanna Brooks was to continue as his singing partner for the foreseeable future, didn't he?"

"Who told you that?"

"It's been corroborated."

Carol's confident tone convinced Corinne. "All right, " she said sulkily. "So he said that. So what? He'd have changed his mind the next day."

"He was dead, then."

The intentionally brutal words brought tears to Corinne's eyes. As she turned her face away, Carol said gently, "Were you lovers?"

The truculence had gone from her voice. "Yes—until the last month or so, when he wouldn't have anything to do with me."

Appalled, Carol thought, *He didn't tell you that you could be HIV-positive . . .* She said, "Do you know why he changed?"

There was pain in her voice. "I couldn't get him to talk to me. He said he'd tell me later, but he never did."

Carol was torn between the desire to warn her,

and relief that she couldn't. She said, "You didn't leave the concert and go to see him at the hotel to discuss why he'd changed his mind?"

Corinne sat down, putting her face in her hands. "What was the use? He wouldn't discuss anything . . . I think he'd begun to hate me . . ."

Carol resisted the impulse to comfort her. She murmured a few platitudes, then escaped into the warm Sunday morning, her thoughts about Collis Raeburn savage. Guilt had made him cruel; pride and arrogance had kept him silent.

She went into work to find Mark already there, looking incongruously young in a sports shirt and shorts. He followed her into her office waving the photograph of Raeburn in the gay bar. "Bingo," he said. "Turned up two of these guys last night."

"And?"

"And Collis Raeburn was a regular. Called himself Col and, I gather, was regarded as being a risk-taker. Sniffed a bit of cocaine, but wasn't a heavy user. He'd try any new designer drug that was around, just for kicks. Lot of sexual partners—as long as they were good-looking and young, he didn't care who they were."

"Graeme Welton ever on the scene?"

Bourke grinned. "We think as one, Carol, but in this case to no avail. Had Welton's photo shown around the bars last night, but no one recognized him. Any relationship he had with Raeburn was strictly private."

"And Amos Berringer?"

"Madeline Shipley was absolutely right. We couldn't find him, but he's still around, trying to keep a low profile. The little prick's too stupid to keep totally quiet, but all he's saying is that he's got some money for keeping his mouth shut and he knows where to get some more."

"Bring him in, Mark."

"The payoff's probably from Kenneth Raeburn, trying to plug the leaks."

"It could be someone else. Let's find out."

"Almost forgot," said Mark. "You haven't had time to read the Sunday papers, I suppose? No? Well you're going to be very interested in an item of gossip. Hold on, I'll get it for you."

Mark had circled it in heavy black ink. Under the heading SINGING AND SUING? the columnist declared, "An impeccable source tells me that all is not well in the Eureka Opera Company. Hit by the tragic loss of Collis Raeburn last week, the company is reeling as top prima donna Alanna Brooks threatens legal action against her leading man, Lloyd Clancy, citing defamation and slander. Is this the end of Edward Livingston's dream of an opera company for the twenty-first century?"

"It's all that deep breathing when they sing," said Bourke. "It drives them mad."

Carol sent Mark home, went out for a brief lunch, then spent the best part of the afternoon wading through the paperwork that had all but buried the in-tray.

Aunt Sarah called to say that David had

inveigled her into taking him to a movie: "I'm just a pushover for your son, Carol. He's promised me popcorn and a movie about a big dog, so how could I resist?"

Carol was quite aware she wouldn't have resisted either, but she said, "Don't let him talk you into anything else, Aunt. He'll be demanding McDonald's next. I think you'd better put him on so I can straighten him out."

She grinned at David's elaborately casual tone. "Yes, Mum? We're leaving in a minute."

"You're spending the money I gave you, aren't you?" she said with mock severity. "You're not letting Aunt Sarah pay for everything?"

"Oh, Mum!"

Suddenly feeling weak with love for him, she said softly, "Darling, have a good time. I wish I were going with you."

A few minutes later the phone rang again. "You work too hard, Carol," Madeline Shipley said. "I just caught your aunt and she said you were there. I'm at home, alone. Will you call in? Have a drink with me?"

Carol felt an unsettling combination of wariness, grief, indefinable longing, and sexual hunger. "I'm tired, Madeline, and I've got another hour here, at least."

"You're not that tired. It'll only be for a while . . ."

"You just won't give up, will you?" said Carol, with a reluctant smile.

"Never. Carol—"

"Okay. I give in."

Carol's light tone disguised the jolt of excitement

that made her hands unsteady as she replaced the receiver. What was it that made her so cautious? Her natural reserve? Allegiance to Sybil? Suspicion that Madeline could get under her defenses?

She smiled as she said aloud, "Courage, Carol. You're not a virgin." *And maybe,* she thought, *Madeline's only offering a drink . . .*

"Whiskey?"

"Please."

Carol seated herself in a lounge chair and looked around the room with feigned interest. Madeline handed her a cut-glass tumbler and sat down opposite. "Tell me about Sybil."

Carol's chin came up. "There's nothing to say."

"Of course there is, but you don't want to say it. That's all right. It would help, that's all."

Before Carol could give the acerbic reply that would deliver a verbal slap, Madeline added, "Me, Carol. It would help *me.*"

"Help you? How?"

Her eyes were intent. "I'd know the situation. What I was up against."

"I don't want to play games."

Abruptly, Madeline was on her feet, pacing. "It isn't a game, Carol. I'm very serious."

Taking a gulp of her drink, Carol thought, *I should go . . . but I don't want to.* Madeline had moved behind her chair. Without turning her head, Carol said flippantly, "You aren't going to attack me, are you?"

She heard the click as Madeline put her drink

down, then the light touch of hands on her shoulders. "As a matter of fact, I am."

Looking up at her, Carol said severely, "I'm taller than you and I outweigh you. And I'm a police officer. You haven't got a chance."

Madeline's copper hair brushed her cheek. *No,* Carol thought as she willingly lifted her mouth to the kiss. She broke away to say, "I'll spill my whiskey."

There was a tremor in Madeline's voice. "Drink it, Carol. I want to taste it in your mouth."

"This is—"

"Right. You were going to say this is right?"

Carol half laughed, half groaned. "You're implacable. Is it any good putting up a resistance?"

"Only if it's a token one."

Go for it? thought Carol, knowing already the decision was made. She put down her drink, stood, opened her arms.

Madeline kissed her lightly, withdrew. "Do you like to be teased?"

"No."

"Of course you do. You're just not used to it."

Carol was focused on Madeline's curved lips. She wanted to kiss her aggressively, forcefully. To have her respond with compelling ardor. To have her heart race as hers was racing . . .

Madeline stepped back. "Come to bed."

In a dream of passion Carol followed her. She was her center, her focal point, her target. Nothing else mattered.

Madeline was half-laughing, dominant. "Don't undress, Carol. I'm going to make love to you first with your clothes on . . . slide my fingers into your hidden places . . . set you on fire."

Carol, her voice husky, said, "I'm that already."

Madeline chuckled softly, her voice a caress. "It's only a little flame, darling. I'm going to make it a bonfire, so that you're consumed entirely."

She pushed Carol gently against the wall, leaned into her, a knee between her legs, slowly began to unbutton her shirt.

This is so different, thought Carol, shutting her eyes. She suddenly felt free to do anything, say anything, be anything. "Madeline . . ."

"It's all right darling. Let me show you what you really want, what you've always wanted."

Her breath caught at Madeline's touch. The barrier of her clothes was at once an impediment and an excitement. Madeline's mouth was hot against her throat. Hands sliding under her bra, tantalizing with the lightest of contacts. Carol made an inarticulate sound.

"Don't hurry me," said Madeline. "I won't be hurried."

Her touch was soft, maddening, provoking—but never quite enough.

Carol could hardly speak. "This is cruel."

"This is what you want."

Madeline's fingers burned as they entered her. The compulsion of desire licked at her thighs, flamed in her groin. "I've got to lie down."

"No, Carol, you've got to stand up."

Never like this. She couldn't see, could only feel—surging, scalding waves of sensation. "I'll fall."

Madeline's commanding voice whispered against her cheek, "Be brave, darling. You can do it."

Knees locked, head back, moaning with the delight of the pulsing ache that transfixed her, Carol abandoned herself to her body's hunger. And with that submission came deliverance. Held tight in Madeline's arms she shuddered with release. "Oh, God."

"Now you can lie down," said Madeline.

CHAPTER TEN

Carol called an early morning meeting with
Bourke and Anne. It was a relief to concentrate on
her work: whenever she relaxed her guard, burning
thoughts of Madeline, of her own startling
abandonment, dislocated her steadfast image of
herself. And Sybil—she didn't want to consider the
conflicting emotions of guilt and resentment that
resonated there.

"Have you both read *The Euthanasia Handbook*?

Yes? Tell me how you'd make absolutely sure your suicide would be a success."

Anne said, "I'd do everything Collis Raeburn did, except I'd take something to settle my stomach, to make sure I didn't vomit and so not absorb enough drugs to kill me."

"Plastic bag," said Bourke.

Carol nodded. "The author makes the point several times that unless a doctor's actively involved, things can go wrong with drugs. You might fall unconscious before you take enough, or vomit before they're absorbed properly, or you might have some tolerance that means you'd lie there for days until someone finds you still alive."

"So what you do," said Bourke, "is wait until you're almost asleep, pop a plastic bag over your head, tie it round your throat and doze off. Then you suffocate, but you don't know anything about it." He added jocularly, "It's the best way to be dead certain."

"There was no plastic bag," said Anne, "and he choked to death on his own vomit."

Carol spread out the scene-of-crime photographs. "Two things," she said. "First, look how clean he is. The post mortem says there was some half-digested food in his mouth and trachea, but there's nothing on his face or on the pillow. He was unconscious, so how come he's so neat? Second, look at this necktie on the carpet by the end of the bed. What's it doing there? Everything else has been put away and Raeburn's wearing casual clothes, so he doesn't need a tie."

Bourke was frowning over the photographs. "So the murderer uses Raeburn's necktie together with a plastic bag to make sure he dies—but why not leave it over his face? After all, it makes the suicide look even more convincing."

"I don't know," said Carol. "Maybe it looked so bizarre, so horrible, that whoever it was took the plastic bag off once he was dead."

"Tender feelings," said Bourke, "for someone willing to wait around and watch someone slowly die."

Carol could see it in her imagination as vividly as a movie: the grotesque figure on the bed, head bagged and tied at the neck, sucking in the plastic with each struggle for breath . . .

"Okay Anne," she said crisply, "what've you got to report?"

"Nothing on the handbook. We've shown photos to staff at all the likely city bookshops, and the problem is that most people recognize Collis Raeburn, but they're not sure if they've seen him in the shop or in the media. The same with the others. For example, many knew Edward Livingston because he's always getting himself interviewed on TV."

"Glad I'm not famous," said Bourke. "I'd hate to be asked for my autograph as I was fleeing the scene of a crime."

"On that very subject," said Anne, "I showed the set of photographs to all the hotel staff who were on that weekend. That was a no go either, though one guy on reception said he vaguely thought he'd seen one of them during that Saturday evening and he had the impression it was a male. I asked him to go through the photos again, but he couldn't say who it was. Looked down his nose as he told me he sees so many famous people in his job he hardly notices them anymore."

Carol was about to ask for Bourke's report when Anne said, "There's one more thing. I went to the morgue to follow up your idea that someone might have called to check if Raeburn's body had been brought in. Drew a blank, but one of the guys did make a suggestion I'll chase up. He said if he'd been after the information, he'd have called the press reporters rostered on for the night. They cover accidents, hospitals, the morgue, all as a matter of course and they have good contacts who'll tell them what's going on."

Mark Bourke's report was succinct. "Haven't turned up Berringer yet, but we will. While we've been looking for him, one thing of interest's come up—the name of the man who may have given Raeburn HIV. Raeburn had an intense relationship with him for some time a few years ago, then the guy, who was an officer in the army, was posted overseas."

"What's his name?"

"Harris. But it doesn't matter, Carol," said Bourke. "When we chased it up we found he never came back to Australia—died of AIDS six months ago."

Lloyd Clancy lived in an apartment overlooking Manly's modest harbor beach and ferry wharf. He gestured that Carol and Anne should sit on the balcony while he got coffee from the adjoining compact kitchen. The white wrought iron chairs and round table were cold to the touch, but the light breeze was enticingly warm. Looking across the shimmering blue water of Manly Cove, they could see Monday morning commuters thronging the wharf, newspapers and briefcases at the ready, waiting to board the sleek jetcats or one of the stately older ferries for the trip to Sydney.

"What a great way to start a working day—half an hour of sitting in the sun on a ferry looking at the scenery."

As Clancy poured the coffee he smiled at Anne's enthusiasm. "It is most of the time, but you should try it when there's been a storm and your ferry hits the swell coming in from the Heads."

Carol said, "We won't keep you long."

"Meaning you want to get down to business, Inspector?"

Watching him closely, Carol said, "Have you ever been to the hotel where Raeburn died?"

He considered the question calmly. "Yes I have, at least a couple of times. Once was a dinner, the other when I was visiting friends. Why?"

"Recently?"

He seemed unconcerned. "Not recently."

"If it were necessary, would you object to a line-up?"

"Not at all. I'm happy to be in an identification parade, but I must remind you, Inspector, that both I and my colleagues are very well known. We might be identified because someone's seen us on television, for instance."

As he sat back, apparently pleased with this

riposte, Carol said, "Is it true that Alanna Brooks is bringing an action against you?"

He straightened. "I've had reporters ringing me all weekend asking that question."

Curbing her impatience, Carol said, "I'd appreciate the answer."

He played with his spoon, then looked up to meet Carol's steady gaze. "I've tried to speak to Alanna, but she's not taking my calls. It's some misunderstanding about last Saturday night."

"At the Museum of Modern Art? You were both there for Andrew Rath's exhibition and reception, weren't you?"

"Yes, and I'm afraid I had too much to drink. I knew I was catching the Manly ferry home and wasn't driving, so I didn't watch how much I had." He chuckled ruefully. "I said some unfortunate things about Alanna, and I'm sorry now, but I suppose it's too late."

"Could you be more explicit?"

"Have you spoken to her?"

Carol let her impatience show. "We're speaking to *you.*"

The clear morning light pitilessly revealed the dark circles under his eyes, the deep lines that bracketed his mouth, the tremor in his hand as he picked up his coffee cup. All the vitality that Carol had seen on the stage and in his dressing room seemed to have drained away. He cleared his throat. "From what I remember, and what I've been told, I suggested, among other things, that Alanna got to be prima donna by a series of underhand maneuvers, including calling in favors and paying off Livingston and other members of the board of Eureka Opera. I said she was worried Corinne would displace her, so she took action to make sure that didn't happen."

"Why would anyone take this seriously? You said you'd had too much to drink . . ."

He swallowed a mouthful of coffee. "It was *who* I spoke to, rather than just what I said. Andrew Rath's an institution in Australian art, so every cultural critic was there at some time in the evening. I managed to find four critics who were having a lively discussion and make them the audience for my comments about Alanna. No one was stupid enough to print it, thank God, but obviously the word's finally got back to her." He gave a tired smile. "To say the least, she's not happy, and she's threatening to sue me for slander."

Carol frowned. "Does this seem to be an overreaction to you?"

He leaned back, shaking his head. "Collis's death has upset everyone. We're all under pressure. I've tried to talk some sense into Alanna, but . . ." His shrug conveyed her lack of cooperation.

Anne said, "Won't that make it difficult when you sing in the same opera?"

Amusement flickered across his face. "You'd be surprised how many love duets are sung by people who loathe each other. From a professional point of view, the audience should never know what we really feel."

"What do you really feel?"

Carol's terse question sobered him immediately. "About what?"

"Alanna Brooks."

He spread his hands. "I don't know . . . resentful, I suppose, that she should take what I said so seriously."

"I've been told you were lovers."

He didn't react for a moment, then he said, "It wasn't Corinne that said this, was it? She's always got an ax to grind."

"It wasn't Ms Jawalski."

"Well, it's not true, Inspector." He paused, apparently to see whether Carol would respond. She didn't. He said uncomfortably, "Look, I don't want to embarrass Alanna, but she made it clear a while ago that she was interested in me. I didn't return her feelings, and told her so as gently as I could."

"Was this before or after she had an affair with Collis Raeburn?"

He flushed. "I don't know anything about that, but I can't believe that she did. Alanna'd have better taste." He sat forward. "Who's been telling you this?"

"I'm sorry . . ."

Lloyd Clancy laughed contemptuously. "Don't tell me—you can't reveal your grubby little sources! Do you believe every bit of gossip anyone tells you?"

"No," said Carol. "Only the ones that check out."

Walking back to the car, Anne said, "Who was you grubby little source?"

"Douglas Binns the night we saw *Aida,* and he doesn't strike me as grubby at all . . ."

As soon as she walked into her office she was given a series of messages, each more urgent than

169

the last, all from Nicole Raeburn. Feeling a mixture of irritation and curiosity, she was about to pick up the receiver when the phone rang.

"Carol Ashton."

"What have I done to deserve that sharp tone?" said Madeline.

In spite of herself, Carol heard her voice mellow as she said, "I thought you'd be on your way to Brisbane by now."

"The plane's delayed, so I'm still at the airport. Queensland, the California of Australia, will have to wait a little longer for me." Carol heard her take a breath, then she said, "How are you feeling, sweetheart?"

"Fine."

Madeline laughed. "Only fine? What happened to fantastic, terrific and wonderful?"

Her body tingling with an echo of passion, she said calmly, "All those too, of course."

"I should wrap up the Queensland segments by next Monday. I'll call you when I get back."

"Yes, okay."

Her amusement plain, Madeline said, "Don't bother sweeping me off my feet with enthusiasm, Carol. I have enough for both of us."

A light blinked on her handset. "I've got another call, Madeline. I'll have to go."

Nicole Raeburn's voice shrieked in her ear. "Inspector! I've been trying to get you all morning. There are two things I *must* know. The first is about your report. When's it going to be finished?"

"The investigation isn't complete yet."

Carol's patient tone obviously inflamed, rather than calmed. "That's what you said last time I asked! All you have to say is that he died accidentally! It's the best thing for everyone, and it's true!"

Carol was tempted to break the connection, but she held her temper and said neutrally, "What was the second thing, Ms Raeburn?"

Nicole's voice suddenly developed a cajoling tone. "Actually, Inspector, it's about Colly's journal. I wondered if you'd found it?"

Carol's negative reply pushed Nicole's voice a notch higher. "You have to find it!"

"Ms Raeburn, why is the journal suddenly so important?"

Her tone became confidential. "Actually, I don't want this to get out, but I'm talking to a well-known writer about Colly's biography, and he says he needs everything personal, though of course I'll decide what goes into the book. And there'll be a lot from me, too . . ."

Collis wasn't the only one in the family with a monstrous ego. "You and your brother were very close . . ."

This gained a complacent agreement.

"Would he have minded if you'd glanced at his journal?"

There was a pause. "I did, once."

Carol waited.

"Inspector Ashton, I hope you don't think . . ."

"Of course not." Her soothing words were an encouragement.

Nicole said, "Colly wrote what he really thought about people, and the secrets they told him they didn't want repeated . . ."

"How long ago was this, when you glanced at the

book?" Carol smiled to herself over "glanced"—she was sure Nicole would have avidly read it.

"A few months ago. I didn't mean to do it, I just happened to see it . . ."

"So you didn't see it recently?"

"Well . . ." A little girl voice. "I think Colly knew I'd peeked. He started locking the journal in his desk, or taking it with him."

Carol's tone was one of mild interest. "So he might have had it with him in the hotel?"

"It isn't *here*. I've looked everywhere, so Colly must've taken it with him."

"We didn't find it in the hotel room."

"Where is it, then?" said Nicole petulantly.

Carol didn't want to give her a chance to embark upon a fruitless conversation about the whereabouts of the journal, as she was sure whoever had killed Raeburn had taken it. She said, "When you did read a little of it, was there anything in particular you remember?"

"Yes," said Nicole triumphantly. "He said Alanna Brooks was a bitch. That she was just using him."

"I don't quite understand."

Nicole was angry with Carol's obtuseness. "She was sleeping with Colly. Taking advantage of him. She didn't care about him at all, but at first he thought she did."

"They were having an affair?"

"I just told you so!" Nicole snapped. Then, changing to a note of complaint, "Is it any wonder Colly was so upset he didn't know what he was doing? That's why he took too many pills—she made

him so unhappy and angry. If you like, she killed
him!"

Douglas Binns was anxiously contrite. "Inspector,
I'm afraid Miss Brooks is still in the rehearsal room
walking through her movements for *Turandot.*" He
coughed apologetically. "You could wait in her
dressing room . . ."

"Would you take us to the rehearsal room,
please."

He hesitated, then said, "Of course."

Carol and Anne followed him through the
familiar low-roofed wide corridors, across the Green
Room and down a flight of stairs to a large
octagonal room with a high ceiling and mirrored
walls. Colored plastic tape laid in patterns lined the
polished wooden floor. Alanna Brooks was deep in
conversation with a small dark-haired man.

"That's the conductor," said Binns in a hushed
voice. He seemed to want to keep them occupied so
they wouldn't interrupt what he obviously considered
an important conversation. He indicated the tape on
the floor. "There's a different color for each opera.
Singers have to know the positions of the flats in
each scene, and, of course, where the doors are."
Seeing Anne blinking at a large sign which declared,
extraordinarily, NO JUMPING AFTER 7:30, he
added, "This rehearsal room's sandwiched in the
middle—the Concert Hall's above us, and the Drama
Theater's below . . ."

173

Carol left him with Anne and strode over to Alanna Brooks, who looked up, startled, as she approached. She muttered an excuse to the conductor, then advanced to meet Carol. "Inspector Ashton? I told Douglas I'd be delayed."

"It's necessary I speak with you immediately."

Alanna's voice was polite, her expression strained. "Of course. Do you want to go to the Green Room, or my dressing room?"

"Somewhere private."

The narrow window of the dressing room poured dazzling light into their eyes. With a muttered comment, Alanna pulled curtains across to block the glare. "Please sit down." She licked her lips. "Now, what is it?"

Carol waited until Anne had notebook and pen ready, then she said, "We interviewed Lloyd Clancy this morning."

Alanna sat very still. "Yes?" she said.

"Why did you wait so long before threatening to take some action against him? You must have known last weekend what he'd said on Saturday night."

"Inspector, I didn't know then. I saw you after *Aida* on Friday, then went on to a party. James Kant was there and he told me what Lloyd had said—it was the first I'd heard."

James Kant was a well-known opera and theater critic and had been one of the four Lloyd Clancy had accosted at the Museum of Modern Art; Carol had no doubt he would corroborate her story. "Do you mean to take Mr. Clancy to court, or is it just a threat to shut him up?"

Alanna narrowed her eyes. "I'm not sure what

174

you're implying. I don't need to shut him up, as you put it."

Carol said pleasantly, "So this is a serious matter, from your point of view?"

"It's obvious it is."

Ignoring the edge in Alanna's voice, Carol said, "It seems you didn't tell me the truth about your relationship with Collis Raeburn."

Her expression didn't change, but she straightened in the chair. "I believe I did."

"I have it on good authority that during the last year you were lovers. Is that true?"

"No."

Carol raised her eyebrows fractionally. The silence hung in the room. At last Alanna said, "We weren't exactly *lovers*. I went to bed with him a couple of times, that's all."

I can hardly ask if you used condoms... "Why did you lie before?" Carol's slight emphasis on "lie" made Alanna flinch.

Alanna said earnestly, "It didn't seem relevant. And I didn't want to think about it. It was a stupid thing to do and Collis only despised me for it." She looked for some sign of acceptance. "That's why I didn't want to say anything."

Another pause which Carol deliberately let last until even Anne shifted in her chair. Alanna said, almost desperately, "Is that all? I've got to get back..."

"Is there anything else you haven't been completely truthful about?"

"I don't believe so."

"Lloyd Clancy?"

Her expression hardened. "About Lloyd," she said firmly, "I've been absolutely truthful. I don't usually hate people, but with Lloyd I could make an exception."

Anne waited until they'd been cleared by security at the stage door entrance. "Do you think she's telling the truth?"

"Partly."

Anne fished her sunglasses out of her bag. "I'd hate to be the person to have to tell Raeburn's lovers that he might have given them HIV—but somebody has to."

Carol nodded, thinking of Pat James's younger brother. "I think the news will be out soon." As Anne looked at her with surprise, she added, "An arrest for murder should do it."

"Inspector Ashton . . . Carol," said Sykes, smiling winningly.

Carol looked stonily at his sleek, self-satisfied face. "Mr. Sykes?"

"As a matter of good PR, I think the time's right for a statement on your progress with the investigation. I'm afraid the news about Alanna Brooks suing her leading man has stirred things up. I've spoken to Eureka Opera's public relations person, and she agrees we need some damage control here."

"We?"

He looked taken aback at her tone. "It's a matter of cooperation. Eureka has been besieged by the media, just as we have. Collis Raeburn's funeral is on Thursday and that'll be, I fully expect, an international media event. It would be advantageous if you could indicate something definite by Wednesday."

"You want the whole case neatly tied up and presented by Wednesday?"

"Not the full written report, of course, but an indication . . ."

"The Commissioner sent you to say this?"

Even Sykes was not immune to Carol's contemptuous anger. He flushed as he said, "Not exactly. After all, it *is* my area—public relations, that is."

Carol had a sudden thought. "Has Kenneth Raeburn been talking to you?" She didn't need his reply, his expression was enough. "And is Mr. Raeburn insisting that I find his son's death was an accident?"

"He believes it was."

"Thank you, Mr. Sykes."

He didn't accept her dismissal. "Inspector Ashton, I don't want you to think I'm trying to tell you how to do your job . . ."

"No?" said Carol caustically. "Then just what *are* you trying to do?"

She expected the phone call from Kenneth Raeburn. "Inspector Ashton, I'd like to see you."

"I'm sorry, Mr. Raeburn, but I'm on a very tight schedule. Could we discuss it on the phone?"

"Not really."

You bastard. You think there's a chance this call

might be recorded. "Could you give me some indication?"

"I'm concerned about your investigation, Inspector. It's ten days since my son's body was discovered and you seem no closer to establishing that it was an accident. As you know, the funeral is in two days, there'll be a great deal of publicity, and people will want answers."

"I'm afraid an investigation doesn't run to a set agenda, so it's impossible to predict exactly when it will end."

"I insist on seeing you tomorrow. It won't be necessary for me to take this higher, will it, Inspector?"

Carol controlled her anger, ignored his last question and made a time to see him.

She sat frowning after the call. Was there any point in going to the Commissioner?

"To hell with it!" she said, startling Anne, who had paused in the doorway. "Yes, Anne?"

"Simon Sykes gave me this media release for you to vet. He didn't want to see you himself, just asked if you'd glance at it and make any changes."

Carol smiled cynically. "You know," she said, "I think Simon Sykes might be just a little scared of me."

CHAPTER ELEVEN

When Carol got up early the next morning, David, in rumpled pajamas, was already in the kitchen. "Mum, can I stay with you and Auntie Sarah for the rest of the week?"

"Darling, I'm on a case, so I may not see that much of you." Expecting his pout, she smiled when it appeared. "All right, I'll ask your father. He's back tonight and Eleanor was going to pick you up tomorrow, but I'll see what I can do."

"Can I come on the run with you?"

She rumpled his blond hair. "If you hurry."

David kept up with her for the first ten minutes, then began to fall behind. She slowed to a walk as they reached the bush path. "Do you run the whole way, Mum?"

"Yes, but I do it every morning, that's why I can."

"If I lived with you, *I* could do it too."

Warmed by his words, she put an arm around his shoulders. "Aren't you happy with your father and Eleanor?"

"Yes. But I like being with you."

"David, I love having you here and you can come as often as you like, you know that."

He looked up at her. "Why's Sybil gone away?"

Say something direct, Carol. You owe him that much.

"You know how your Dad and Eleanor love each other—how they do things together, sleep in the same room..."

"Well, they're married, Mum," he said, making it clear this was self-evident.

"Sybil and I are like that... it's just like we're married."

"Then why's she moved out?"

"Because we're not getting on at the moment. We've got some problems we're trying to work out."

David looked sideways at her for a long moment. Then he said, "Can we start jogging again?"

That's enough. It's a beginning.

"Sure," said Carol, "but I bet you can't keep up."

* * * * *

180

While David was dressing for school, Carol had breakfast with Aunt Sarah, who frowned at Carol's toast and black coffee, but managed not to give her usual lecture on health foods. Carol defiantly poured herself a second cup of coffee, ignoring her aunt's muttered comment. "I said something on the run this morning about Sybil and me. If David asks you any questions, please answer them."

"He won't, Carol. David must have picked up something from Justin's casual remarks or assumptions made about you and Sybil being together . . . that sort of thing. Now you've given David a bit more to think about. He'll fit it all together, and when he's ready, he'll ask you what he wants to know."

"I may not have the luxury of waiting—Kenneth Raeburn's leaning on me."

"What about the calls on your answering machine?"

"I know who made those," she said with dour satisfaction. "But that's not necessarily much help."

Aunt Sarah patted her hand. "If you're outed, you're outed," she said. "And there's probably nothing you can do about it."

Carol wanted the relief of losing her temper, breaking something, screaming her rage. Instead she said calmly, "Except to find that Collis Raeburn's death was an accident. That would take the heat off."

"At least you've got a choice."

"You know, my dear Aunt, that I haven't."

"Tsk," said Aunt Sarah. "Principles are such a curse."

* * * * *

Kenneth Raeburn had insisted that they meet outside her office. "I'm staying at the Park Royal. It'd be more convenient if we met in the foyer."

Carol was early, and had brought Anne with her. Kenneth Raeburn, chest out, standing as tall as possible, was already there. He frowned when he saw the constable. "I'm sorry. What I have to say is confidential. There can be no third party."

Edgy and impatient, he still spoke in his usual soft half-whisper. Although his well-cut dark suit was appropriate to the hotel's elegance, his broken nose and insolent stare seemed incongruous. "Well?" he demanded.

Carol directed Anne to wait out of earshot, then sat down with him on a plush lounge. "Why is this confidential? Constable Newsome is assisting the investigation and is quite aware of all developments."

His gesture dismissed her comment. "I don't want to waste time. I expect you to find that Collis died by a combination of unfortunate circumstances. It was not suicide, not murder, but an accident."

Carol was equally terse. "You're not in a position to dictate the results of my investigation."

"What would it hurt you to come to this conclusion?" His voice, almost inaudible, shook with tension. "The mere suggestion of anything else will ensure that the inquest is a circus, and will destroy his memory, not to mention what it will do to Nicole."

"I'm afraid I can't take any of that into consideration. I'm only concerned with the truth."

"The truth?" he sneered. "You don't tell the truth about yourself . . ."

Carol wanted to hit him. She said in a controlled voice, "This has nothing to do with me personally. I've got a job to do, and I'm doing it."

"It's a matter of your arrogance, Inspector. You refuse to see his death as a sad, unnecessary accident. You want it to be murder, because that gives you so much more publicity, doesn't it? You're in this for your own glory, so don't pretend to have any high ideals."

"There's no point in continuing this conversation."

Raeburn nodded to himself, as though satisfied with her hostile response. "Don't leave. You'll want to hear what I have to say."

"Mr. Raeburn, attempting to influence a police officer is a criminal offense."

He laughed contemptuously. "Don't give me that. You must know I'll deny everything, and frankly, I don't imagine you're recording this. You know what I'm going to say, and you'd hardly want your colleagues to hear it."

"There's nothing you *can* say that will change my findings one way or the other."

"No? I've had you investigated by a discreet and very expensive private detective. You live with a Sybil Quade, who was a suspect in one of your cases. Now she's your lover." He paused for her reaction. When her expression didn't change he said contemptuously, "Detective Inspector Carol Ashton, closet lesbian. Is that why you're persecuting Collis's memory? Because you think he was queer, and you hate that in him, as you must in yourself?"

Armored by her icy rage, Carol said, "Did you encourage your daughter to leave threatening messages on my answering machine, or was it her own idea?"

"I'm not here to answer questions. I'm here to tell you what it would be very wise for you to do."

He rose from the lounge as she did, looking up at her with venomous intent. "Let me make you a promise, Inspector. Unless you find that his death was an accident, you'll face the consequences. You ruin Collis's reputation—I'll ruin yours."

"This better be urgent," said the Commissioner. "I've rescheduled an appointment with the Minister because of you."

Even though the Commissioner had previously given his full public and personal support to gay and lesbian police officers when a splinter group had attempted to out them, Carol still felt a stinging apprehension as she said evenly, "Kenneth Raeburn is trying to blackmail me into making a report that presents his son's death as an accident."

"Blackmail you? How?"

Carol put the miniature tape player on his desk. "I had an idea that's what he was going to do, so I was wired. Constable Newsome observed our meeting, but wasn't within earshot." She pressed the play button and sat down. Raeburn's voice was soft, but clear. Without comment they listened through to the end.

She didn't expect his response. "Sybil Quade, eh? The Bellwether murders?"

"Yes."

Frowning, he rested his chin on his steepled fingers. "You're not denying what he says?"

She met his gaze directly. "About being a lesbian? No." She needed to say something more. "But that's my private life. It has nothing to do with my job."

"It shouldn't have anything to do with it, you mean." He rubbed a hand over his face. "Tough it out, Carol."

"You don't think I'm compromised? You're not taking me off the case?"

The Commissioner looked irate. "Because of Kenneth Raeburn? Hell, no." He gave her a slight smile. "Or because you're gay? Hell no, again."

She returned his smile, her respect for him at a new level.

As she turned to go, he said, "Want my advice? Have Bourke threaten to charge Raeburn with trying to pervert the course of justice—that should shut him up for a while. If you're sure about the daughter, suggest she might be charged too. And close the murder case as fast as you can. It'll be out of Raeburn's hands then and he's not as likely to cause trouble for you, or for himself. Basically what I'm saying, Carol, is if you can make an arrest, make it now."

* * * * *

She called Bourke and Anne into her office. "Close the door, Mark. I want you and Anne to listen to a tape of my conversation this morning with Kenneth Raeburn. I've already played it to the Commissioner."

Her voice seemed to convey some of the stress she was feeling. Bourke glanced at her soberly, then sat down without his usual jesting comment. Anne, who had seen Carol's silent white-faced rage after the meeting at the Park Royal, avoided eye contact altogether.

They listened to the tape without comment. The click when she turned off the recorder sounded loud in the silence. Bourke leaned over and put his hand over hers. "Carol . . ." After a moment he released her. His expression hardened. "We can get Raeburn for that."

"The Commissioner suggests threatening him with trying to pervert the course of justice."

"It'll be a pleasure."

"I'm sure Nicole Raeburn left the messages on my answering machine—in conversation with me she used phrases that occurred on the tape."

Bourke was delighted. "I'll mention charging her, too. That should wipe the smiles off their faces."

Anne still hadn't looked up. Carol said, "Mark knows about my personal life, Anne, so this isn't a surprise for him."

Carol realized, as Anne finally met her glance, that it was anger, not embarrassment or disdain, reflected on the young constable's face. "It isn't fair. That little bastard shouldn't be able to use it against you."

186

Carol could hear the resignation in her own voice as she said, "It had to happen one day."

"How do we handle it?" said Bourke.

Carol had thought this through. "People in the Service will know, and that means there's a good chance the fact I'm a lesbian will go further. And, of course, there's Raeburn and his daughter, the private detective they used . . ."

"You could deny everything."

"I could, Anne, but then I'm just reactive, and at a disadvantage. I want to have some sort of control here. The Commissioner knows, and so will my other superiors after this meeting. Aside from that, I'm not making any statements to anyone, but if I'm asked a direct question, I'll answer it directly."

"What do you want us to do?"

She sighed. "Mark, what do I say to you? It's up to you what you say or don't say."

Anne said, "What about the media?"

Carol smiled grimly. "I haven't quite decided. Frankly, I hope I don't have to, but I'm inclined to think that 'yes, so what?' may be the way to go."

Bourke stood. "I'm off to intimidate Kenneth Raeburn," he said cheerfully, rubbing his hands together. "And believe me, I'm looking forward to it."

Carol called the college where Sybil taught part-time. After an interminable delay, she felt her heart jump as she heard Sybil's familiar voice. "It's me."

"Carol? What's wrong?"

"Does something have to be wrong?"

"For you to ring me at work—yes."

As she told her what had happened, Carol was conscious that Sybil might welcome what she, herself, dreaded. What might represent freedom to Sybil meant loss of control to Carol.

Sybil said, "I'll come back home."

"No, don't," she said involuntarily.

There was a long pause, then, "You don't want me there?"

"It's not that—"

"What is it, then, Carol? Worried that my presence will confirm the gossip? That people will come round to see for themselves?"

"I don't need this!"

Sybil was immediately calm. "No, you don't. I'll stay away, Carol, but we need to talk. Do you agree?"

"Yes, of course."

Sybil's voice was husky. "I love you. I don't want you hurt, and I don't want to cause you any more problems. Call you tonight, okay?"

Carol shut her eyes, confused by guilt, love and misery. "Okay," she said.

CHAPTER TWELVE

Early on Wednesday morning Bourke bounded into Carol's office. "We got Berringer. A little worse for wear."

"He put up a fight?"

"Hardly. What he *did* do was try to shake Kenneth Raeburn down over Collis' homosexuality. I'd say Raeburn wanted to flush Berringer out of the woodwork, so he arranged to pay him off. Berringer won't say how much it was, and he didn't have it long. He had time to boast a bit about how smart he'd been, then two very large gentlemen gave him a very painful going over and, to add insult to injury, took the money back. That was enough to send Berringer straight into hiding." He grinned with obvious pleasure as he added, "Our Kenneth didn't take at all kindly to my visit yesterday, so I imagine he's going to be even more unhappy today after I mention including him in possible assault charges when we pick up his goons."

Carol showed her doubt. "What credibility would this Berringer character have in court against someone like Kenneth Raeburn?"

"Very little," said Bourke agreeably, "but I'm going to have fun suggesting it's a possibility. This should shut Raeburn up quite effectively."

"Anne called in a few minutes ago. She's found a cub reporter on the *Sentinel* who fielded a telephone inquiry about whether Collis Raeburn was dead, but it was on *Sunday,* before his body'd been found. The journalist was just a kid, and didn't realize there might be something worth following up."

"Don't suppose the person left a name?"

Without pleasure Carol said, "No, Mark, but it was a woman. Also, I called Pat at work this morning and asked her some questions about the Saturday night reception at the Museum of Modern Art."

He raised his eyebrows. "Helpful?"

"I think we're near an arrest. I'd like you and Anne in my office at two."

"Come in, Inspector. We've been waiting for you."

Carol felt like an interloper, guarded on one side

by Mark Bourke and by Anne Newsome on the other. She said formally, "Thank you for agreeing to a joint interview."

Alanna went to stand beside Lloyd Clancy. Behind them, through the open balcony doors, the blue water of Manly Cove shimmered in the afternoon sun. Carol felt a pang of pity and compassion as she saw Alanna take Lloyd Clancy's hand and hold it tightly.

Lloyd Clancy gestured, the thoughtful host. "Please, make yourselves comfortable."

Alanna and Clancy sat beside each other on a couch, still holding hands. Carol thought of all the roles these two had taken, where intense, flamboyant emotions were translated into glorious music. She remembered *Aida* where, as now, they were doomed lovers. This was an anticlimax, this real drama ending so mundanely in a harborside apartment.

"You know why we're here," Carol said with quiet authority.

Alanna looked at her steadily. "Yes, we do."

"Do you object to us recording this interview?"

Alanna shook her head slowly, and Bourke efficiently set up the tape recorder on the coffee table. He nodded to Carol to indicate he was ready. She took no pleasure in reciting the formal words of the caution, adding to make sure they understood, "You don't have to say anything now if you don't wish to."

"It's quite all right," Alanna said. "It'll be a relief, actually."

Bourke said, "Collis Raeburn didn't kill himself. He was murdered in a way that was intended to look like suicide."

191

Lloyd Clancy sighed. "I'll save you the trouble of spelling it out. I can't imagine how to say this without sounding overly dramatic, but I killed Collis. No one helped—it was just me."

Carol said with real regret, "That's not true."

"Sweetheart, don't," Alanna said to Clancy. "I'm sure the Inspector knows."

Lloyd was haggard, but his look to Alanna was so full of love that Carol almost winced. She said, "You went to a lot of trouble to make people think you hated each other."

"We thought it would stop any suspicion that we might be working together," said Alanna. She looked embarrassed. "The idea of threatening to sue Lloyd was my idea, but it was over the top, I see that now."

"Why did you make the phone calls to check if Raeburn was dead? You knew he was."

"*Lloyd* knew," said Alanna, "but *I* didn't. We couldn't be seen anywhere near each other at the reception, that would have been too dangerous. And we'd agreed not to use the telephone because there might be a record of the calls. I kept on thinking that Collis might be lying there, still alive, and if he were to recover . . ." She made a face. "It was stupid, but I had no idea when the hotel would open the room, and I was frantic to know if he was dead. I tried the newspaper, but drew a blank. When nothing had been in the news by early Monday morning, I tried the hotel."

Lloyd Clancy coughed painfully.

Bourke said, "You're not well, Mr. Clancy. Can I get you some water?"

He smiled faintly. "I think it's the flu, but of course I keep thinking it's something worse . . ."

"When did you realize that Collis Raeburn had infected Ms Brooks, and through her, you?"

Alanna answered. "Collis finally got up the courage to tell me six weeks ago. It took a while to sink in that I was probably going to die from AIDS. And when I found that I'd infected Lloyd . . . that's when the rage began . . . that's when I knew I wanted to exterminate Collis."

Anne Newsome said faintly, "There's treatment for AIDS . . ."

Alanna nodded wearily. "Yes, Sergeant, of course we've both had the latest medical advice, but my immune system is seriously compromised, and Lloyd's T-cell count is falling." She laughed bitterly. "You know, even though he'd been infected longer, Collis was doing better than either of us. He'd had pneumonia, but seemed to recover well. AIDS affects everyone differently, but that didn't seem fair to me."

Lloyd Clancy said, "Collis didn't care, Inspector. He never said he was sorry because he couldn't see he'd done anything wrong. Bad luck, he called it. And he was sure *he'd* be all right . . . Thought he had a charmed life."

"Why did you kill him?"

Alanna answered. "I asked him if he'd told others he'd slept with—Corinne for example—and he said he wasn't going to, that he'd only told *me* because of old times and because he knew I couldn't tell anyone else without ruining my own life."

"He was an egotistical monster," said Lloyd. "Collis really believed that, for him, ordinary rules and standards didn't apply, and other people were there for his use. And now he'd condemned us both. Alanna's — *my* life is singing. Opera's demanding, exhausting. We both realized it would be only a matter of time before one or both of us couldn't continue. We decided to kill him for what he'd done to us . . . and would continue to do to others."

He rubbed his face wearily and Carol suggested they stop for coffee or tea. The recorder was switched off and Lloyd Clancy, Anne and Bourke went to the kitchen. Alanna said to Carol, "Inspector, you understand, don't you?"

"I think I do, yes."

"What will happen to us?"

What a pair of amateurs these two are, Carol thought. She was sure Alanna would reject pity, so she said matter-of-factly, "Plead not guilty at the committal hearing and apply for bail. I'll do everything I can to see that you get it. That way you can spend more time together."

"With a bit of luck," said Alanna with mordant humor, "we might die before we ever come to trial."

When they resumed, Alanna seemed to have new energy. "We used a duplicate checklist. We knew we couldn't make any mistakes. Lloyd and I went separately to the reception in the Museum of Modern Art and we each made sure we spoke to as many people as possible. I had a large shoulder bag with me—not the sort I usually carry, but I had to hide cotton gloves, a bottle of whiskey and the suicide handbook in it. I knew the sleeping tablets Collis used—we'd been lovers, after all—and I'd managed to get a doctor to prescribe the same brand for me. I crushed more than half of them, dissolving them as much as possible until they made a solution which I put in an old medicine bottle. The other half I kept in tablet form in case Collis hadn't brought any with him, but he had, so in the end I didn't need them."

She grimaced. "It sounds bizarre describing it like this, but at the time it seemed like the script of a movie—not quite real, but logical and right. About eight o'clock I slipped out of the Museum and walked the few minutes to the hotel. I'd spoken to Collis in the afternoon and he'd told me he had his usual room, so I went up the fire stairs to his floor. He was surprised to see me, but he'd just finished a bottle of wine and he was quite relaxed. Actually, Collis was feeling proud of himself because he'd called Corinne and told her I was staying on as his singing partner. I remember he said, 'See, I'm making it up to you' and that made me so angry that I really wanted to kill him. He'd infected me with the HIV virus and he thought this would make it up to me! I smiled and showed him the bottle of Johnny Walker Black Label. It was always his favorite drink—and he was quite happy to have me serve him. While I was getting ice from the bar fridge I poured some of the solution into his glass. He said it didn't taste quite right, but I pointed out he'd just eaten tuna and he was a bit tipsy, so he kept drinking. I just pretended to sip mine . . ."

Her voice trailed off. To encourage her, Bourke said, "And he didn't suspect anything was wrong?"

Her mouth twisted. "He'd never think I'd be a threat to him. Do you know what we talked about? The treatment he was having for the virus. The new drugs he'd had sent from overseas. He told me how great it was to be able to discuss it with someone who understood. I was glad he was saying these things because it made it so much easier for me. He started to get sleepy and I persuaded him to lie on the bed. He was still talking, slurring his words, when Lloyd knocked in a code we'd agreed on. I put on the cotton gloves and let him in. Collis was very vague, but he still wanted to know what Lloyd was doing there, though he didn't seem to mind when we didn't answer. Lloyd put on his gloves and I gave him the sleeping tablet solution and the copy of *The Euthanasia Handbook* in its plastic wrap. Then I washed the glass I'd used and checked my list to make sure I'd done everything."

Carol said, "Did you take his journal?"

Alanna flushed with anger. "It was open on the table because he'd been writing in it. When I left I took it, because I thought it might mention me and Lloyd."

"Did it?"

"I've burnt the journal, Inspector, but I'm glad I read it. It made me sure that we were doing the right thing."

"You put the Do Not Disturb on the door?"

"Yes. Then I went back to the Museum. I'd been away for a bit over an hour, but there were so many people there I was fairly sure I hadn't been missed, and I made sure I was seen from then on."

"Now it's my narrative," said Lloyd with a sketchy attempt at a smile. "It was just after nine when I ordered coffee and had all calls to the room stopped. Naturally it was assumed I was Collis. I waited until the coffee was left outside, poured him a cup, added some of Alanna's solution and held it while he had some. As soon as he was completely unconscious I took out my checklist and put it on the bedside table so I wouldn't forget anything. I remember thinking how awful it would be if I killed him, shut the door behind me, then remembered the list was still there . . . Anyway, I wiped the whiskey bottle and his glass, in case Alanna had touched either of them, and put his fingerprints on each of them. I took the handbook out of its plastic and did the same with it. By now he was breathing in great, slow, snoring gasps . . . it was horrible and I wanted him to stop. I took the plastic bag I had folded in my pocket, found one of his neckties, and put the bag over his head and tied it."

"You got all these details from the handbook?"

He sighed at Bourke's question. "In the book it sounded so clinical. I hadn't realized how awful it would be, Collis lying there with his head wrapped in plastic and the heat of his breath steaming it up inside. He coughed and made a choking noise. He was lying completely still and I waited for him to start breathing again, but he didn't. I made sure I hadn't left anything, picked up the list and checked the room about three times. And then I looked at him and it was horrible, him with his head in a bag. I saw he'd vomited, and though I hated him, I couldn't leave him like that. I took off the tie and stuffed it in my pocket, then eased off the plastic bag—the air in it was hot, so damp and smelly and I thought I'd vomit too. Collis was dead, but I found I just had to wash his face. Dampened one of his handkerchiefs and cleaned him up, put the handkerchief with the plastic bag and the book wrapping in my pocket, tipped over the glass of whiskey and scattered the pills across the carpet. I left his bottle of painkillers in the bathroom cabinet and I took any other medication he had."

His smile was completely without humor. "Alanna and I thought, you see, that there was no reason for anyone to discover he was HIV-positive, unless they found Collis had drugs to treat it."

Carol said gently, "It's standard in a post mortem to do a blood test for it."

"We didn't know that. There were a lot of things we didn't take into account."

"You dropped the tie," said Carol, almost regretfully.

"Yes, I was in such a hurry to get out of there—I was panicking because I couldn't stand to be in the room with him. I turned on the television and the air-conditioning, and I ran. The tie wasn't in my pocket when I chucked everything else into a litter bin, but of course I couldn't go back because I had to leave his key inside the room."

"Tell me," said Carol with real curiosity, "did you arrange him so his hand was draped artistically?"

Lloyd looked down, obviously embarrassed. "I'm afraid I did. It didn't look right to me, the way he was lying. I thought it would be more convincing the way I arranged it."

That's the trouble, thought Carol, *you were trying too hard to be certain it looked like suicide...*

Later, over subdued case-closed drinks at the nearest pub, Bourke said, "No wonder they caved in, Carol. Your manner even convinced me you knew every detail—and I knew you didn't."

Anne added her own admiring nod.

Carol swirled the whiskey in her glass. "I was sure two people were involved because of the phone calls. Obviously, whoever waited for Raeburn to die, then removed the plastic bag from his head, knew the murder was successful ... so who was the second person ringing the paper and the hotel manager to make certain?"

Anne said, "Someone who wasn't sure Raeburn was dead."

"Yes, Anne, but why would you not know he was dead? The person must have left the hotel room before Raeburn died and then had no way of finding out exactly what had happened. This meant there must be some reason why these two people would make strenuous efforts not to be linked together—so I was looking for a couple who had a strong joint motive, but who appeared to be quite separate from each other."

"Right," Anne said, "but why did it have to be Lloyd Clancy and Alanna Brooks?"

"Look at any other possible combination. Raeburn and his daughter?"

"Supportive of each other," supplied Bourke.

Carol nodded. "Nicole and Welton—they're friends who even saw me together. And who and why would anyone want to combine with Corinne Jawalski?"

"Well, what about Welton and Livingston?" argued Anne. "Welton attacked Edward Livingston, and they both had a motive over *Dingo*."

Again Carol nodded, pleased with the young constable. "It was a possibility, but the motive didn't seem strong enough. Other combinations, such as Raeburn with Welton, didn't work either. But Lloyd and Alanna did." She ticked off her points. "They had the opportunity—the reception they attended was near Raeburn's hotel and Pat told me it was very crowded, with people coming and going all night. They had the motive. Although Alanna had renewed her relationship with Collis, she denied it after his death because she knew of his HIV status and that she was infected. She also denied, as did Lloyd, that they had had a relationship—why bother to do this unless they had something to hide?"

"And both of them attacked each other to show how alienated they were," said Anne, raising her wineglass in salute to Carol.

Bourke grinned at Anne. "Mind like a steel trap, Constable. Make a detective out of you yet." He grew more serious as he said to Carol, "Collis Raeburn's sex partners are in for an awful shock when this hits the papers—and there's no way that it won't."

"Yes," Carol said grimly, thinking about Corinne Jawalski, Graeme Welton and Edward Livingston, and hoping that the horrific toll of this virus would not end up taking in the entire Eureka Opera Company.

Mark said softly to Carol, "The word's filtered down to me not to press charges as far as Kenneth Raeburn's concerned, which will keep your name out of the media, Carol."

"For the moment," she said dryly.

Anne's indignation was plain. "He shouldn't get away with it!"

"He hasn't," said Bourke, "his whole world's blown up in his face and his precious son's reputation with it." He touched his beer mug to Carol's glass as he added, "You know, we cops close ranks over some things—no one's going to be talking to the media about you."

Carol sipped her whiskey, inspecting this new shift in the center of her universe. She was out now, to her own family and to her police family. She was no fool—there would be problems, serious ones. But it felt right. And good. Very good indeed...

"Oh God!" she said suddenly. "Talking about the media reminds me of Simon Sykes. He demanded I tie up the case by Wednesday and now I've bloody well done it to his schedule..."

CHAPTER THIRTEEN

Balmoral Beach looked ravishing in the bright spring day. Little waves danced in from the harbor, seagulls inspected the sand or wheeled overhead with flashing white wings, a few swimmers braved the chill of the water while the less adventurous paced along the yellow sand. Up from the sea wall the white rotunda sat smugly in a sea of lawn.

Carol smiled at Mark Bourke, whose usual nonchalance had abandoned him. "I know something's going to go wrong, Carol."

"Relax. It's pre-wedding nerves."

Knots of people were gathering, greeting each other with lighthearted comments. The marriage celebrant beckoned. "Mark, we'll be starting in a moment."

Carol gave him a gentle shove. "Go on, Pat's waiting for you."

As he went up to take his place Carol saw Sybil's red hair. Carol skirted the crowd and came up beside her. Carol said, "Hello, darling."

Sybil gave her a tentative smile. As Carol took her hand, linking their fingers, she had a sudden flash of Alanna and Lloyd holding hands. She said, "Are you coming home?"

Sybil tightened her fingers. "Maybe. Can you give me a good reason to?"

"I miss you."

"Not bad, but have you something better?"

"Jeffrey really misses you."

"That," said Sybil, "just might do it."

A few of the publications of
THE NAIAD PRESS, INC.
P.O. Box 10543 • Tallahassee, Florida 32302
Phone (904) 539-5965
Mail orders welcome. Please include 15% postage.

THE EROTIC NAIAD edited by Katherine V. Forrest & Barbara Grier.
224 pp. Love stories by Naiad Press authors.   ISBN 1-56280-026-4 $12.95

DEAD CERTAIN by Claire McNab. 224 pp. 5th Det. Insp. Carol
Ashton mystery.   ISBN 1-56280-027-2   9.95

CRAZY FOR LOVING by Jaye Maiman. 320 pp. 2nd Robin
Miller mystery.   ISBN 1-56280-025-6   9.95

STONEHURST by Barbara Johnson. 176 pp. Passionate regency
romance.   ISBN 1-56280-024-8   9.95

INTRODUCING AMANDA VALENTINE by Rose Beecham.
256 pp. An Amanda Valentine Mystery — 1st in a series.
                                                 ISBN 1-56280-021-3   9.95

UNCERTAIN COMPANIONS by Robbi Sommers. 204 pp.
Steamy, erotic novel.   ISBN 1-56280-017-5   9.95

A TIGER'S HEART by Lauren W. Douglas. 240 pp. Fourth Caitlin
Reece Mystery.   ISBN 1-56280-018-3   9.95

PAPERBACK ROMANCE by Karin Kallmaker. 256 pp. A
delicious romance.   ISBN 1-56280-019-1   9.95

MORTON RIVER VALLEY by Lee Lynch. 304 pp. Lee Lynch at
her best!   ISBN 1-56280-016-7   9.95

LOVE, ZENA BETH by Diane Salvatore. 224 pp. The most talked
about lesbian novel of the nineties!   ISBN 1-56280-015-9   18.95

THE LAVENDER HOUSE MURDER by Nikki Baker. 224 pp. A
Virginia Kelly Mystery. Second in a series.   ISBN 1-56280-012-4   9.95

PASSION BAY by Jennifer Fulton. 224 pp. Passionate romance,
virgin beaches, tropical skies.   ISBN 1-56280-028-0   9.95

STICKS AND STONES by Jackie Calhoun. 208 pp. Contemporary
lesbian lives and loves.   ISBN 1-56280-020-5   9.95

DELIA IRONFOOT by Jeane Harris. 192 pp. Adventure for Delia
and Beth in the Utah mountains.   ISBN 1-56280-014-0   9.95

UNDER THE SOUTHERN CROSS by Claire McNab. 192 pp.
Romantic nights Down Under.   ISBN 1-56280-011-6   9.95

RIVERFINGER WOMEN by Elana Nachman/Dykewomon.
208 pp. Classic Lesbian/feminist novel.   ISBN 1-56280-013-2   8.95

BLACK IRIS by Jeane Harris. 192 pp. Caroline's hidden past . . .
ISBN 0-941483-68-1   8.95

TOUCHWOOD by Karin Kallmaker. 240 pp. Loving, May/
December romance.   ISBN 0-941483-76-2   8.95

BAYOU CITY SECRETS by Deborah Powell. 224 pp. A Hollis
Carpenter mystery. First in a series.   ISBN 0-941483-91-6   8.95

COP OUT by Claire McNab. 208 pp. 4th Det. Insp. Carol Ashton
mystery.   ISBN 0-941483-84-3   9.95

LODESTAR by Phyllis Horn. 224 pp. Romantic, fast-moving
adventure.   ISBN 0-941483-83-5   8.95

THE BEVERLY MALIBU by Katherine V. Forrest. 288 pp. A
Kate Delafield Mystery. 3rd in a series. (HC)   ISBN 0-941483-47-9   16.95
Paperback   ISBN 0-941483-48-7   9.95

THAT OLD STUDEBAKER by Lee Lynch. 272 pp. Andy's affair
with Regina and her attachment to her beloved car.
ISBN 0-941483-82-7   9.95

PASSION'S LEGACY by Lori Paige. 224 pp. Sarah is swept into
the arms of Augusta Pym in this delightful historical romance.
ISBN 0-941483-81-9   8.95

THE PROVIDENCE FILE by Amanda Kyle Williams. 256 pp.
Second espionage thriller featuring lesbian agent Madison McGuire
ISBN 0-941483-92-4   8.95

I LEFT MY HEART by Jaye Maiman. 320 pp. A Robin Miller
Mystery. First in a series.   ISBN 0-941483-72-X   9.95

THE PRICE OF SALT by Patricia Highsmith (writing as Claire
Morgan). 288 pp. Classic lesbian novel, first issued in 1952 . . .
acknowledged by its author under her own, very famous, name.
ISBN 1-56280-003-5   8.95

SIDE BY SIDE by Isabel Miller. 256 pp. From beloved author of
Patience and Sarah.   ISBN 0-941483-77-0   9.95

SOUTHBOUND by Sheila Ortiz Taylor. 240 pp. Hilarious sequel
to *Faultline.*   ISBN 0-941483-78-9   8.95

STAYING POWER: LONG TERM LESBIAN COUPLES
by Susan E. Johnson. 352 pp. Joys of coupledom.
ISBN 0-941-483-75-4   12.95

SLICK by Camarin Grae. 304 pp. Exotic, erotic adventure.
ISBN 0-941483-74-6   9.95

NINTH LIFE by Lauren Wright Douglas. 256 pp. A Caitlin
Reece mystery. 2nd in a series.   ISBN 0-941483-50-9   8.95

PLAYERS by Robbi Sommers. 192 pp. Sizzling, erotic novel.
ISBN 0-941483-73-8   9.95

MURDER AT RED ROOK RANCH by Dorothy Tell. 224 pp.
First Poppy Dillworth adventure.   ISBN 0-941483-80-0   8.95

LESBIAN SURVIVAL MANUAL by Rhonda Dicksion.
112 pp. Cartoons! ISBN 0-941483-71-1 8.95

A ROOM FULL OF WOMEN by Elisabeth Nonas. 256 pp.
Contemporary Lesbian lives. ISBN 0-941483-69-X 8.95

MURDER IS RELATIVE by Karen Saum. 256 pp. The first
Brigid Donovan mystery. ISBN 0-941483-70-3 8.95

PRIORITIES by Lynda Lyons 288 pp. Science fiction with
a twist. ISBN 0-941483-66-5 8.95

THEME FOR DIVERSE INSTRUMENTS by Jane Rule. 208
pp. Powerful romantic lesbian stories. ISBN 0-941483-63-0 8.95

LESBIAN QUERIES by Hertz & Ertman. 112 pp. The questions
you were too embarrassed to ask. ISBN 0-941483-67-3 8.95

CLUB 12 by Amanda Kyle Williams. 288 pp. Espionage thriller
featuring a lesbian agent! ISBN 0-941483-64-9 8.95

DEATH DOWN UNDER by Claire McNab. 240 pp. 3rd Det.
Insp. Carol Ashton mystery. ISBN 0-941483-39-8 9.95

MONTANA FEATHERS by Penny Hayes. 256 pp. Vivian and
Elizabeth find love in frontier Montana. ISBN 0-941483-61-4 8.95

CHESAPEAKE PROJECT by Phyllis Horn. 304 pp. Jessie &
Meredith in perilous adventure. ISBN 0-941483-58-4 8.95

LIFESTYLES by Jackie Calhoun. 224 pp. Contemporary Lesbian
lives and loves. ISBN 0-941483-57-6 9.95

VIRAGO by Karen Marie Christa Minns. 208 pp. Darsen has
chosen Ginny. ISBN 0-941483-56-8 8.95

WILDERNESS TREK by Dorothy Tell. 192 pp. Six women on
vacation learning "new" skills. ISBN 0-941483-60-6 8.95

MURDER BY THE BOOK by Pat Welch. 256 pp. A Helen
Black Mystery. First in a series. ISBN 0-941483-59-2 8.95

BERRIGAN by Vicki P. McConnell. 176 pp. Youthful Lesbian —
romantic, idealistic Berrigan. ISBN 0-941483-55-X 8.95

LESBIANS IN GERMANY by Lillian Faderman & B. Eriksson.
128 pp. Fiction, poetry, essays. ISBN 0-941483-62-2 8.95

THERE'S SOMETHING I'VE BEEN MEANING TO TELL
YOU Ed. by Loralee MacPike. 288 pp. Gay men and lesbians
coming out to their children. ISBN 0-941483-44-4 9.95
ISBN 0-941483-54-1 16.95

LIFTING BELLY by Gertrude Stein. Ed. by Rebecca Mark. 104
pp. Erotic poetry. ISBN 0-941483-51-7 8.95
ISBN 0-941483-53-3 14.95

ROSE PENSKI by Roz Perry. 192 pp. Adult lovers in a long-term
relationship. ISBN 0-941483-37-1 8.95

AFTER THE FIRE by Jane Rule. 256 pp. Warm, human novel
by this incomparable author.   ISBN 0-941483-45-2   8.95

SUE SLATE, PRIVATE EYE by Lee Lynch. 176 pp. The gay
folk of Peacock Alley are *all cats*.   ISBN 0-941483-52-5   8.95

CHRIS by Randy Salem. 224 pp. Golden oldie. Handsome Chris
and her adventures.   ISBN 0-941483-42-8   8.95

THREE WOMEN by March Hastings. 232 pp. Golden oldie. A
triangle among wealthy sophisticates.   ISBN 0-941483-43-6   8.95

RICE AND BEANS by Valeria Taylor. 232 pp. Love and
romance on poverty row.   ISBN 0-941483-41-X   8.95

PLEASURES by Robbi Sommers. 204 pp. Unprecedented
eroticism.   ISBN 0-941483-49-5   8.95

EDGEWISE by Camarin Grae. 372 pp. Spellbinding
adventure.   ISBN 0-941483-19-3   9.95

FATAL REUNION by Claire McNab. 224 pp. 2nd Det. Inspec.
Carol Ashton mystery.   ISBN 0-941483-40-1   8.95

KEEP TO ME STRANGER by Sarah Aldridge. 372 pp. Romance
set in a department store dynasty.   ISBN 0-941483-38-X   9.95

HEARTSCAPE by Sue Gambill. 204 pp. American lesbian in
Portugal.   ISBN 0-941483-33-9   8.95

IN THE BLOOD by Lauren Wright Douglas. 252 pp. Lesbian
science fiction adventure fantasy   ISBN 0-941483-22-3   8.95

THE BEE'S KISS by Shirley Verel. 216 pp. Delicate, delicious
romance.   ISBN 0-941483-36-3   8.95

RAGING MOTHER MOUNTAIN by Pat Emmerson. 264 pp.
Furosa Firechild's adventures in Wonderland. ISBN 0-941483-35-5   8.95

IN EVERY PORT by Karin Kallmaker. 228 pp. Jessica's sexy,
adventuresome travels.   ISBN 0-941483-37-7   9.95

OF LOVE AND GLORY by Evelyn Kennedy. 192 pp. Exciting
WWII romance.   ISBN 0-941483-32-0   8.95

CLICKING STONES by Nancy Tyler Glenn. 288 pp. Love
transcending time.   ISBN 0-941483-31-2   9.95

SURVIVING SISTERS by Gail Pass. 252 pp. Powerful love
story.   ISBN 0-941483-16-9   8.95

SOUTH OF THE LINE by Catherine Ennis. 216 pp. Civil War
adventure.   ISBN 0-941483-29-0   8.95

WOMAN PLUS WOMAN by Dolores Klaich. 300 pp. Supurb
Lesbian overview.   ISBN 0-941483-28-2   9.95

SLOW DANCING AT MISS POLLY'S by Sheila Ortiz Taylor.
96 pp. Lesbian Poetry   ISBN 0-941483-30-4   7.95

DOUBLE DAUGHTER by Vicki P. McConnell. 216 pp. A Nyla
Wade Mystery, third in the series.   ISBN 0-941483-26-6   8.95

HEAVY GILT by Delores Klaich. 192 pp. Lesbian detective/
disappearing homophobes/upper class gay society.
ISBN 0-941483-25-8   8.95

THE FINER GRAIN by Denise Ohio. 216 pp. Brilliant young
college lesbian novel.   ISBN 0-941483-11-8   8.95

THE AMAZON TRAIL by Lee Lynch. 216 pp. Life, travel & lore
of famous lesbian author.   ISBN 0-941483-27-4   8.95

HIGH CONTRAST by Jessie Lattimore. 264 pp. Women of the
Crystal Palace.   ISBN 0-941483-17-7   8.95

OCTOBER OBSESSION by Meredith More. Josie's rich, secret
Lesbian life.   ISBN 0-941483-18-5   8.95

LESBIAN CROSSROADS by Ruth Baetz. 276 pp. Contemporary
Lesbian lives.   ISBN 0-941483-21-5   9.95

BEFORE STONEWALL: THE MAKING OF A GAY AND
LESBIAN COMMUNITY by Andrea Weiss & Greta Schiller.
96 pp., 25 illus.   ISBN 0-941483-20-7   7.95

WE WALK THE BACK OF THE TIGER by Patricia A. Murphy.
192 pp. Romantic Lesbian novel/beginning women's movement.
ISBN 0-941483-13-4   8.95

SUNDAY'S CHILD by Joyce Bright. 216 pp. Lesbian athletics, at
last the novel about sports.   ISBN 0-941483-12-6   8.95

OSTEN'S BAY by Zenobia N. Vole. 204 pp. Sizzling adventure
romance set on Bonaire.   ISBN 0-941483-15-0   8.95

LESSONS IN MURDER by Claire McNab. 216 pp. 1st Det. Inspec.
Carol Ashton mystery — erotic tension!.   ISBN 0-941483-14-2   8.95

YELLOWTHROAT by Penny Hayes. 240 pp. Margarita, bandit,
kidnaps Julia.   ISBN 0-941483-10-X   8.95

SAPPHISTRY: THE BOOK OF LESBIAN SEXUALITY by
Pat Califia. 3d edition, revised. 208 pp.   ISBN 0-941483-24-X   8.95

CHERISHED LOVE by Evelyn Kennedy. 192 pp. Erotic
Lesbian love story.   ISBN 0-941483-08-8   9.95

LAST SEPTEMBER by Helen R. Hull. 208 pp. Six stories & a
glorious novella.   ISBN 0-941483-09-6   8.95

THE SECRET IN THE BIRD by Camarin Grae. 312 pp. Striking,
psychological suspense novel.   ISBN 0-941483-05-3   8.95

TO THE LIGHTNING by Catherine Ennis. 208 pp. Romantic
Lesbian 'Robinson Crusoe' adventure.   ISBN 0-941483-06-1   8.95

THE OTHER SIDE OF VENUS by Shirley Verel. 224 pp.
Luminous, romantic love story.   ISBN 0-941483-07-X   8.95

DREAMS AND SWORDS by Katherine V. Forrest. 192 pp.
Romantic, erotic, imaginative stories.   ISBN 0-941483-03-7   8.95

MEMORY BOARD by Jane Rule. 336 pp. Memorable novel
about an aging Lesbian couple.   ISBN 0-941483-02-9   9.95

THE ALWAYS ANONYMOUS BEAST by Lauren Wright
Douglas. 224 pp. A Caitlin Reece mystery. First in a series.
                                         ISBN 0-941483-04-5   8.95

SEARCHING FOR SPRING by Patricia A. Murphy. 224 pp.
Novel about the recovery of love.   ISBN 0-941483-00-2   8.95

DUSTY'S QUEEN OF HEARTS DINER by Lee Lynch. 240 pp.
Romantic blue-collar novel.   ISBN 0-941483-01-0   8.95

PARENTS MATTER by Ann Muller. 240 pp. Parents'
relationships with Lesbian daughters and gay sons.
                                         ISBN 0-930044-91-6   9.95

THE PEARLS by Shelley Smith. 176 pp. Passion and fun in
the Caribbean sun.   ISBN 0-930044-93-2   7.95

MAGDALENA by Sarah Aldridge. 352 pp. Epic Lesbian novel
set on three continents.   ISBN 0-930044-99-1   8.95

THE BLACK AND WHITE OF IT by Ann Allen Shockley.
144 pp. Short stories.   ISBN 0-930044-96-7   7.95

SAY JESUS AND COME TO ME by Ann Allen Shockley. 288
pp. Contemporary romance.   ISBN 0-930044-98-3   8.95

LOVING HER by Ann Allen Shockley. 192 pp. Romantic love
story.   ISBN 0-930044-97-5   7.95

MURDER AT THE NIGHTWOOD BAR by Katherine V.
Forrest. 240 pp. A Kate Delafield mystery. Second in a series.
                                         ISBN 0-930044-92-4   9.95

ZOE'S BOOK by Gail Pass. 224 pp. Passionate, obsessive love
story.   ISBN 0-930044-95-9   7.95

WINGED DANCER by Camarin Grae. 228 pp. Erotic Lesbian
adventure story.   ISBN 0-930044-88-6   8.95

PAZ by Camarin Grae. 336 pp. Romantic Lesbian adventurer
with the power to change the world.   ISBN 0-930044-89-4   8.95

SOUL SNATCHER by Camarin Grae. 224 pp. A puzzle, an
adventure, a mystery — Lesbian romance. ISBN 0-930044-90-8   8.95

THE LOVE OF GOOD WOMEN by Isabel Miller. 224 pp.
Long-awaited new novel by the author of the beloved *Patience
and Sarah*.   ISBN 0-930044-81-9   8.95

THE HOUSE AT PELHAM FALLS by Brenda Weathers. 240
pp. Suspenseful Lesbian ghost story.   ISBN 0-930044-79-7   7.95

HOME IN YOUR HANDS by Lee Lynch. 240 pp. More stories
from the author of *Old Dyke Tales*.   ISBN 0-930044-80-0   7.95

EACH HAND A MAP by Anita Skeen. 112 pp. Real-life poems
that touch us all.   ISBN 0-930044-82-7   6.95

SURPLUS by Sylvia Stevenson. 342 pp. A classic early Lesbian novel. ISBN 0-930044-78-9   7.95

PEMBROKE PARK by Michelle Martin. 256 pp. Derring-do and daring romance in Regency England. ISBN 0-930044-77-0   7.95

THE LONG TRAIL by Penny Hayes. 248 pp. Vivid adventures of two women in love in the old west. ISBN 0-930044-76-2   8.95

HORIZON OF THE HEART by Shelley Smith. 192 pp. Hot romance in summertime New England. ISBN 0-930044-75-4   7.95

AN EMERGENCE OF GREEN by Katherine V. Forrest. 288 pp. Powerful novel of sexual discovery. ISBN 0-930044-69-X   9.95

THE LESBIAN PERIODICALS INDEX edited by Claire Potter. 432 pp. Author & subject index. ISBN 0-930044-74-6   29.95

DESERT OF THE HEART by Jane Rule. 224 pp. A classic; basis for the movie *Desert Hearts*. ISBN 0-930044-73-8   9.95

SPRING FORWARD/FALL BACK by Sheila Ortiz Taylor. 288 pp. Literary novel of timeless love. ISBN 0-930044-70-3   7.95

FOR KEEPS by Elisabeth Nonas. 144 pp. Contemporary novel about losing and finding love. ISBN 0-930044-71-1   7.95

TORCHLIGHT TO VALHALLA by Gale Wilhelm. 128 pp. Classic novel by a great Lesbian writer. ISBN 0-930044-68-1   7.95

LESBIAN NUNS: BREAKING SILENCE edited by Rosemary Curb and Nancy Manahan. 432 pp. Unprecedented autobiographies of religious life. ISBN 0-930044-62-2   9.95

THE SWASHBUCKLER by Lee Lynch. 288 pp. Colorful novel set in Greenwich Village in the sixties. ISBN 0-930044-66-5   8.95

MISFORTUNE'S FRIEND by Sarah Aldridge. 320 pp. Historical Lesbian novel set on two continents. ISBN 0-930044-67-3   7.95

A STUDIO OF ONE'S OWN by Ann Stokes. Edited by Dolores Klaich. 128 pp. Autobiography. ISBN 0-930044-64-9   7.95

SEX VARIANT WOMEN IN LITERATURE by Jeannette Howard Foster. 448 pp. Literary history. ISBN 0-930044-65-7   8.95

A HOT-EYED MODERATE by Jane Rule. 252 pp. Hard-hitting essays on gay life; writing; art. ISBN 0-930044-57-6   7.95

INLAND PASSAGE AND OTHER STORIES by Jane Rule. 288 pp. Wide-ranging new collection. ISBN 0-930044-56-8   7.95

WE TOO ARE DRIFTING by Gale Wilhelm. 128 pp. Timeless Lesbian novel, a masterpiece. ISBN 0-930044-61-4   6.95

AMATEUR CITY by Katherine V. Forrest. 224 pp. A Kate Delafield mystery. First in a series. ISBN 0-930044-55-X   9.95

THE SOPHIE HOROWITZ STORY by Sarah Schulman. 176 pp. Engaging novel of madcap intrigue. ISBN 0-930044-54-1   7.95

THE YOUNG IN ONE ANOTHER'S ARMS by Jane Rule. 224 pp. Classic
Jane Rule.   ISBN 0-930044-53-3   9.95

THE BURNTON WIDOWS by Vickie P. McConnell. 272 pp. A
Nyla Wade mystery, second in the series.   ISBN 0-930044-52-5   9.95

OLD DYKE TALES by Lee Lynch. 224 pp. Extraordinary
stories of our diverse Lesbian lives.   ISBN 0-930044-51-7   8.95

DAUGHTERS OF A CORAL DAWN by Katherine V. Forrest.
240 pp. Novel set in a Lesbian new world.   ISBN 0-930044-50-9   8.95

AGAINST THE SEASON by Jane Rule. 224 pp. Luminous,
complex novel of interrelationships.   ISBN 0-930044-48-7   8.95

LOVERS IN THE PRESENT AFTERNOON by Kathleen
Fleming. 288 pp. A novel about recovery and growth.
                                              ISBN 0-930044-46-0   8.95

TOOTHPICK HOUSE by Lee Lynch. 264 pp. Love between
two Lesbians of different classes.   ISBN 0-930044-45-2   7.95

MADAME AURORA by Sarah Aldridge. 256 pp. Historical
novel featuring a charismatic "seer."   ISBN 0-930044-44-4   7.95

CURIOUS WINE by Katherine V. Forrest. 176 pp. Passionate
Lesbian love story, a best-seller.   ISBN 0-930044-43-6   8.95

BLACK LESBIAN IN WHITE AMERICA by Anita Cornwell.
141 pp. Stories, essays, autobiography.   ISBN 0-930044-41-X   7.95

CONTRACT WITH THE WORLD by Jane Rule. 340 pp.
Powerful, panoramic novel of gay life.   ISBN 0-930044-28-2   9.95

MRS. PORTER'S LETTER by Vicki P. McConnell. 224 pp.
The first Nyla Wade mystery.   ISBN 0-930044-29-0   7.95

TO THE CLEVELAND STATION by Carol Anne Douglas.
192 pp. Interracial Lesbian love story.   ISBN 0-930044-27-4   6.95

THE NESTING PLACE by Sarah Aldridge. 224 pp. A
three-woman triangle — love conquers all!   ISBN 0-930044-26-6   7.95

THIS IS NOT FOR YOU by Jane Rule. 284 pp. A letter to a
beloved is also an intricate novel.   ISBN 0-930044-25-8   8.95

FAULTLINE by Sheila Ortiz Taylor. 140 pp. Warm, funny,
literate story of a startling family.   ISBN 0-930044-24-X   6.95

ANNA'S COUNTRY by Elizabeth Lang. 208 pp. A woman
finds her Lesbian identity.   ISBN 0-930044-19-3   8.95

PRISM by Valerie Taylor. 158 pp. A love affair between two
women in their sixties.   ISBN 0-930044-18-5   6.95

THE MARQUISE AND THE NOVICE by Victoria Ramstetter.
108 pp. A Lesbian Gothic novel.   ISBN 0-930044-16-9   6.95

OUTLANDER by Jane Rule. 207 pp. Short stories and essays
by one of our finest writers.   ISBN 0-930044-17-7   8.95

ALL TRUE LOVERS by Sarah Aldridge. 292 pp. Romantic
novel set in the 1930s and 1940s.   ISBN 0-930044-10-X   8.95

A WOMAN APPEARED TO ME by Renee Vivien. 65 pp. A
classic; translated by Jeannette H. Foster.   ISBN 0-930044-06-1   5.00

CYTHEREA'S BREATH by Sarah Aldridge. 240 pp. Romantic
novel about women's entrance into medicine.
                                                ISBN 0-930044-02-9   6.95

TOTTIE by Sarah Aldridge. 181 pp. Lesbian romance in the
turmoil of the sixties.   ISBN 0-930044-01-0   6.95

THE LATECOMER by Sarah Aldridge. 107 pp. A delicate love
story.   ISBN 0-930044-00-2   6.95

ODD GIRL OUT by Ann Bannon.   ISBN 0-930044-83-5   5.95
I AM A WOMAN 84-3; WOMEN IN THE SHADOWS 85-1;   each
JOURNEY TO A WOMAN 86-X; BEEBO BRINKER 87-8. Golden
oldies about life in Greenwich Village.

JOURNEY TO FULFILLMENT, A WORLD WITHOUT MEN, and   3.95
RETURN TO LESBOS. All by Valerie Taylor   each

These are just a few of the many Naiad Press titles — we are the oldest and
largest lesbian/feminist publishing company in the world. Please request a
complete catalog. We offer personal service; we encourage and welcome direct
mail orders from individuals who have limited access to bookstores carrying
our publications.